**"You're rushing me, Jean-Claude,"
Sherry said uneasily. "Can't we
take it one step at a time?"**

"One step at a time? Then I suppose the first step is to be certain you will stay for the entire recording session. And the next step is to ask if you will join me for lunch. And after that, perhaps we might spend the afternoon together. And after that, dinner."

"Wait!" She laughed. "That sounds like three or four steps to me."

He pulled a face of mock chagrin. "Ah, you noticed!"

She chuckled and shook her head. "Jean-Claude, you're impossible."

"Impossible to resist, I hope."

She pursed her lips and made herself look prim. "Nothing is impossible, Jean-Claude."

Purposely misunderstanding her, he leered. "Nothing? You give me great hope, Chérie."

Kerry Price

Kerry Price's first love has always been books—reading and now writing them—but her second love, music, has given her a rewarding career as a classical percussionist. She plays frequently with the Los Angeles Philharmonic, for visiting opera and ballet companies, and for movies and TV. She spent a year on the road with the New York Shakespeare Festival's production of The Pirates of Penzance, not only playing percussion, but also acting "bits," which, she confesses, she thoroughly enjoyed.

One of the relatively few women percussionists, Kerry has the even rarer distinction of being a genuine Southern California native. Currently, she lives in the San Fernando Valley, where she shares a house with two Australian shepherds named Chubby and Ellen. Her first marriage ended in divorce and her second husband died. She describes herself as "still hoping to meet a man as devastatingly attractive as my fictional heroes."

Kerry perceives music and writing as basically similar. "Both require a drop of inspiration and barrels of perspiration," she says. "As in practicing an instrument, the more one writes, the better one gets. I hope to go on practicing my writing for a long, long time."

Dear Reader:

It takes a darn fine writer to capture the emotional acrobatics of two creatively frustrated, romantically cautious, and generally mischievous housemates as vividly—and endearingly—as Laine Allen does in *Tangling With Webb* (#346). Historical romance writer Cristy McKnight is tired of quivering virgins and dastardly villains; spy thriller author Webb Cannon has had it with slick undercover operatives and faithless female double agents. In a quirky about-face, Cristy and Webb reverse writing roles ... and soon both they *and* their fictional creations are caught in the stickily complicated—and suddenly sensual—web of this uproarious tale.

Next, I'm thrilled to introduce our latest SECOND CHANCE AT LOVE "discovery," new author Kerry Price, whose light, sparkling *Frenchman's Kiss* (#347) presents Jean-Claude Delacroix, a hero no woman could resist. Spunky Sherry Seaton is knocked off-balance when the sexy, charming, thoroughly enticing Frenchman sweeps her into a world of sophisticated glamour and whimsical fun. It all begins with what Sherry mistakenly assumes is an obscene phone call. Further complications arise when she meets Jean-Claude at a hotel room during a blackout—and he takes full advantage of the situation's sensual possibilities! Jean-Claude's methods may be madness, but he's irresistible—and so is *Frenchman's Kiss*.

In *Kid at Heart* (#348), Aimée Duvall returns with all the zest and zaniness you've come to expect. Here, wacky toy designer Lisa Fleming and company owner Chase Sanger team up to invent a new line of playthings ... and discover they'd rather fool around with each other. Who'd think a sophisticated, urbane guy like Chase could become such an uninhibited, fun-loving playmate? But Lisa seems to attract confusion, and Chase has a hard time maintaining his businesslike demeanor when confronted with a robot gone berserk or a group of appallingly inventive six-year-olds—not to mention his own eccentric family. In *Kid at Heart*, love, and Aimée Duvall, make anything possible!

Helen Carter's latest romance is my personal favorite. She's always a pro at creating complex, deeply sympathetic characters, but in *My Wild Irish Rogue* (#349) she surpasses her previous accomplishments with a prim and proper sociologist heroine and a carefree, pleasure-seeking (but never irresponsible!) hero. In Liam Clare, Helen combines Irish charm and American ingenuity, masculine strength and penetrating insight, to form a perfect hero—one who challenges Ingrid to open herself to new possibilities, to forget statistics and embrace life—and him!—with passionate energy. But for Ingrid, making such changes is painfully difficult ... *My Wild Irish Rogue* was written soon after Helen's own trip to Ireland, a land that clearly inspired her.

Carole Buck has done it again! Her latest romance, *Happily Ever After* (#350), has more than a fairy-tale ending; it's magical through and through, with all the wit and warmth that have made Carole such a popular SECOND CHANCE AT LOVE writer. The enchantment begins when Lily Bancroft dresses up as Snow White, hoping to wrangle money out of the quellingly authoritative, yet devastatingly masculine man known as the Lone Wolf of Wall Street. How she and Dylan Chase move from antagonism to ardor, achieving a poignant understanding—helped along the way by Dylan's playboy brother and Lily's lovably offbeat friends—forms the stuff of a marvelously inventive, deeply satisfying romance...

Finally, with the emotional power and sensitivity she's known and loved for, Karen Keast tackles one woman's hard-earned bitterness toward men in general and one male in particular. Reluctant Lauren Kane is certain that, if she lets him, sexy Nyles Ryland will become her sensual nemesis. Incorrigible Nyles is intent on proving the same thing—*but* he's gambling Lauren will learn that giving in to her feelings doesn't have to mean defeat, and that her treacherous heart can prove her gentlest ally. The result is *Tender Treason* (#351), a moving story of stormy suspicions, willful seduction, and oh, so sweet surrender.

I hope you enjoy all six of our July releases. And don't forget to drop us a line—we love to hear your thoughts and comments.

Warm wishes,

Ellen Edwards

Ellen Edwards, Senior Editor
SECOND CHANCE AT LOVE
The Berkley Publishing Group
200 Madison Avenue
New York, NY 10016

KERRY PRICE
FRENCHMAN'S KISS

A
SECOND CHANCE AT LOVE
BOOK

FRENCHMAN'S KISS

First edition published July 1986

First printing

"Second Chance at Love" and the butterfly emblem are trademarks
belonging to Jove Publications, Inc.

Printed in the United States of America

Second Chance at Love books are published by
The Berkley Publishing Group
200 Madison Avenue, New York, NY 10016

Chapter 1

SHERRY SEATON TUCKED a long strand of caramel-brown hair behind her ear, picked up the jingling phone, and propped it against her shoulder. "KopyKats."

A streak of lightning raced across the windows lining the office wall. A split-second later, thunder boomed like a giant's drum.

"I'm sorry," Sherry said into the receiver. "I couldn't hear you."

"I said, this is Jean-Claude Delacroix." The baritone voice had a French accent, though only a faint one.

"How can I help you, Mr. Delacroix?"

"I am here in Los Angeles," he announced, as though stating the obvious.

Sherry aimed a puzzled frown at the phone. "Yes, Mr. Delacroix?"

"I have just arrived. How soon can someone be at my hotel?"

Sherry inhaled sharply, her green-flecked hazel eyes flashing with anger. Another nut! Lately, she and her

1

partner, Maggie Rafferty, had been plagued by crank calls. KopyKats' phone number must be posted on the official perverts' bulletin board, she thought.

She had the receiver halfway to the slamming point when she reconsidered. It was just possible the man had simply misdialed. "I'm sorry, sir," she said frostily. "You must have the wrong number. This is a music-copying business."

Without waiting for a response, she hung up, then watched the rain stream down the office windows. For the last few days, January had been doing its impressive worst. Whoever first called California the Golden State hadn't been around for the winter rains, she thought wryly.

She shifted her gaze to the sheet of paper on her desk, on which she had written a list of her monthly expenditures. She couldn't be sure yet, but even without Maggie to share the apartment, she ought to be able to manage the rent. Fortunately, KopyKats had grown into a steady, though modest, source of income.

The phone jangled at her, and she picked up the receiver. "KopyKats."

"We were, I think, cut off," said the lightly accented voice. "Perhaps the storm . . ."

"We weren't cut off. I hung up."

"You hung up? But why?"

Sherry sighed. "Look, Mr. Whatever-your-name-is, this is a music-copying business. We don't provide services that involve going to men's hotel rooms. I suggest you double-check the number you're dialing. Good-bye."

"Wait, I beg you, do not hang up."

"Good-bye," Sherry repeated sweetly, and broke the connection.

Within seconds, the phone rang again. She hesitated, then decided to give it one last chance in case, this time, it was a legitimate customer. "KopyKats."

"Don't hang up." The voice spoke sharply.

Him again. Annoyance made her brusque. "Look, mister, I don't know what game you're playing, but it's gone far enough. There are laws against telephone harassment, you know."

His tone was patient. "I have thought about this difficulty and I have concluded the problem must be my insufficient command of English. Would you please let me try to explain?"

Sherry considered, then said, "All right, I'll listen. But if there's one word about hotel rooms..."

"No hotel rooms, I promise." Amusement colored his voice, making his accent even more appealing. "At least not today. First, I think we should be properly introduced."

"Okay, that does it." With a tight grip on the phone, she prepared for a well-deserved slam in the caller's ear.

"No, no, wait. I am sorry. I must apologize for my misplaced sense of humor." He went on in a rush, "As I told you, my name is Jean-Claude Delacroix. I am a film composer."

Oh, good grief! The man *was* a legitimate customer. "I'm terribly sorry, Mr.—" She broke off abruptly. Something was wrong. Never before had the composer of a film personally telephoned KopyKats; hiring copyists was the job of the film company's music supervisor. "You're looking for a copyist?" she asked warily.

"No, I have a copyist. You. I was told to call this number when I reached Los Angeles. I was also told someone would come to my hotel room..."

There he went with the hotel room bit again. "What company are you working for, Mr. Delacroix?" she asked crisply.

"JRA Films."

Sherry received this information in incredulous silence. If this Delacroix wasn't a nut after all, this was KopyKats' first break into the big time. JRA Films was one of Los Angeles's leading film production companies.

"Listen," she told her caller, "I haven't heard a thing about any job for JRA."

"But I was given this number."

Sherry thought quickly. "When do the recording sessions start? Maybe JRA just hasn't gotten around to calling us yet."

"Wednesday."

"*This* Wednesday?" Her normally low, mellow voice bounded to the flute register. "Two days from now?" Something was definitely fishy. If JRA had intended to hire KopyKats, they would have called days, even weeks, before.

Half-forgetting her caller couldn't see her, she shook her head, her brown hair with its rich caramel tints swaying gently around her shoulders. "I'm sorry, Mr. Delacroix. There must be a mistake. Some other copying firm must be doing your score." Or he was a nut, after all.

"I do not understand." He sounded baffled.

"I don't understand, either. All I can tell you is that KopyKats is definitely not doing the copying for your film." If there really was a film.

"But I am certain . . ."

"But you are wrong, Mr. Delacroix," she said firmly.

There was a long silence; then he said, "Would you mind repeating those words?"

"Repeating . . . ?"

"If you please."

His English must not be as good as it sounded, she decided. "I was trying to explain how impossible it is—"

"I understood you," he broke in. "I merely wanted you to repeat the words you said."

"I don't remember exactly what I said." She was getting annoyed all over again. Since the Frenchman must have mistaken KopyKats for some other firm, why didn't he go about his business?

"You are wrong, Mr. Delacroix," he prompted in a deep, burry voice.

"You are wrong, Mr. Delacroix," she parroted. This was ridiculous! Why was she going along with this nonsense?

"Ah, thank you. Now, my entire name . . ."

Stunned speechless, Sherry gaped at the phone.

"Jean-Claude," he prompted.

He *was* a nut, a certifiable loony. "I think this is where I hang up on you again," she warned.

"No, please. I know you must think—"

"What I think is that I'm saying good-bye now." She plunked down the receiver, then gazed at the phone uneasily. The nut was nothing if not persistent. Any minute now, he'd probably be back on the line. She lifted the receiver from its cradle and laid it on the desk.

Too bad it had turned out to be only a rotten joke, she thought. Working for JRA would have been a giant step for KopyKats. And besides—in spite of everything— she had liked the Frenchman's voice. If he hadn't been a crazy, she would have enjoyed meeting the man who went with that mellow, sexy baritone.

Her mind turned over the thought for a moment; then she glanced back at her interrupted budget calculations. Rent. Car payment. Utilities. It added up to an alarming amount.

Oh, stop worrying! She gave herself a mental shake. She'd come through worse financial straits during her marriage. A little belt-tightening wouldn't hurt her.

The Swedish sleigh bells on the back door of the office jingled sweetly. Maggie Rafferty stepped inside, shaking droplets from her fiery auburn mop like an Irish setter after a bath.

"Boy, it's raining cats and dogs out there!" Maggie folded her dripping umbrella and propped it against the wall.

Sherry smiled. "Only cats and dogs? From in here, it looks more like hippopotamuses and giraffes."

"You have a point." Maggie glanced down the length of the long, neon-lit room and sniffed. "Whew. It smells in here. Have you been running the monster?"

The bulky gray machine and the photocopier beside it had been the partners' major investment when they started KopyKats. The "monster" produced individual musicians' parts in a process much like the one used to make blueprints.

Sherry inhaled. The pungent aroma of photographic fluid filled her nostrils. It was a smell she had enjoyed at first, since it signified KopyKats was alive and functioning. Rent would be paid, food eaten, and clothing worn. But now, the odor seemed unpleasantly medicinal; it clung to her hair and seeped into her clothing.

Sherry suspected that the odor bothered her because of her waxing dissatisfaction with music-copying. Three years back, in the wake of her divorce from Mark, setting up in business with Maggie had seemed like a grand idea. Then, her only goal had been to achieve financial and emotional independence.

Now she had reached that goal. The old dreams of a creative career only surfaced now and again, when melodiés percolated through her head and her fingers itched for the strings of her guitar. Even when she gave in to the itch, her fantasies of being a professional songwriter were firmly under control. KopyKats was a secure reality, and she had no right to complain if the work was sometimes grueling and often tedious.

"Sherry?" Maggie's voice prodded at her.

"I ran off the parts for tomorrow's record date," she explained. "The arranger is picking them up in the morning."

"Then we're all caught up." Maggie hung her raincoat on the old-fashioned coatrack near the door. "Good. I'll need some time to settle in to Jake's apartment." She crossed the room and plopped her petite self onto the edge of Sherry's desk. "Hey! Why's the phone off the hook?"

"Oops! I forgot." Sherry put the earpiece back in place. "Some nut called a while ago. I had to hang up on him."

"Another one of those obscene phone calls?"

"Not exactly. This was a different kind of nut. He—"

The phone jangled. "If that's the nut, I'm going to hang up on him again, I swear it," Sherry vowed. She picked up the phone and said briskly, "KopyKats."

"This is Andrew Watson." The voice was deliberately deep, and decibels too loud. "Is this Ms. Seaton or Ms. Rafferty?"

"This is Sherry Seaton. What can I do for you, Mr. Watson?"

"There's been a slight mix-up in my office, Ms. Seaton." He harrumphed ostentatiously. "Did I mention I'm the music supervisor for JRA Films?"

"No, you didn't." *JRA?* She did a wincing double-take.

"Yes. Fred Wertz over at Sequin Records said you people are fast and accurate."

"We try to be." Her mind raced. Was it possible the nut wasn't a nut after all? That he was exactly who he'd said he was—the composer of the music for a JRA film? It took all her self-control not to groan into Andrew Watson's ear.

He boomed on, "You were supposed to have been contacted weeks ago about copying the music for *Guns and Roses*. Uh . . . you have heard of the project?"

"Yes, Mr. Watson, I've heard of it," she said dryly. She would have had to be lost in the wilds of Borneo *not* to have heard of it. *Guns and Roses,* a recent best-selling novel, was already being touted as a major television epic.

"The problem," Watson blared, "is that our first recording session is Wednesday. Through another mix-up, the composer only arrived in Los Angeles today."

Sherry swallowed. "What's his name?"

"Jean-Claude Delacroix."

The syllables pealed miserably in her ear and she only half heard him go on to list the composer's credits, which included the French art film that had racked up all the prizes at Cannes the year before.

"Remember, the first segment has to be ready by Wednesday morning," Watson cautioned. "You know we can't postpone the session without violating musicians' union rules. Can you people do the job?"

Sherry drew a deep breath. "We'll do it."

"Glad to hear it. Well, there's no time to lose. You'd better get in touch with the composer right away."

"I think I've already spoken with Mr. Delacroix," she said wryly.

"Oh? I won't need to give you his number, then?"

"Yes, you will. I . . . uh, didn't make a note of it when I spoke with him before." She copied down the name and number of a luxury hotel in downtown Los Angeles.

As soon as Andrew Watson hung up, Sherry explained the situation to her partner. When she had finished, Maggie looked as worried as Sherry felt. "Oh, brother. Can we do it?"

"We don't have a choice. We can't turn down JRA. It's going to be rough, though. Uh . . . Maggie," Sherry added slowly. "You know the nut who called before?"

"Yep. What's he got to do with this?"

"The nut was Jean-Claude Delacroix."

"Oh, boy." Maggie winced. "And you hung up on him?"

"Three times."

"Look, partner," Maggie offered, "if you'd rather not deal with him, I'll go pick up his score."

"No, you call the troops. We may as well do it the way we always do." Normally, Maggie hired the assistant copyists they used for large jobs, while Sherry, the better-trained musician, worked with the composer or arranger. "After all, I'd have to confront him sooner or later."

She grabbed her tan raincoat from the coatrack and pulled it over her red knit top and navy slacks. "Call him and let him know I'm on the way," she flung over her shoulder as she stepped out into a torrent of rain. "Tell him I was temporarily deranged but that I'm much better now."

When it rained, everyone in Los Angeles drove at about nine miles an hour. Sherry had noticed the phenomenon before, but had never found it quite as irritating as she did today. By the time she reached the highrise hotel in downtown L.A., it was already dark; the yellow lights of the skyscrapers glimmered weakly through the continuing downpour.

Outside Jean-Claude Delacroix's room on the twenty-first floor, she hesitated, wondering if she should apologize for hanging up on him or leave the subject unmentioned. Not that he deserved an apology. He'd been positively strange, kidding about hotel rooms and asking her to repeat inane sentences for no reason.

She rapped lightly on the wood. Footsteps sounded from inside the room and the door swung open.

Lightning cracked, deafening and very close. Sherry had only a momentary glimpse of wickedly sparkling black eyes in a tanned face before the lights went out.

After an instant of shock-induced paralysis, she lifted her hand in front of her face. Nothing. She might as well be blindfolded.

As she drew two long, steadying breaths, a maddeningly familiar voice spouted something rapid and vehement in French, then finished, "Come in, please."

"All right." She took an incautious step, and her shin hit an object in her path. Off balance, she hurtled forward and crashed into a broad, muscular chest. Strong arms enfolded her, steadied her, and set her on her feet.

She drew a ragged breath. Though he had instantly released her, the impress of a muscular thigh, the flat hardness of a male chest, the warmth of his hands on her waistline felt branded on her body, the sensation unnaturally acute because of her inability to see.

"I . . . I'm sorry," she murmured.

"Do not be sorry." Hints of laughter bubbled in his deep voice. "Do you know, in truth, this is the first time a woman has ever thrown herself into my arms? I shall cherish the memory forever."

"I hate to disappoint you"—she spoke tartly to cover her confusion . . . and her undeniable response to that one dizzying moment in his arms—"but I didn't throw myself anywhere. I tripped over something."

"My briefcase, I imagine."

"Oh." She was tempted to ask what it was doing there, where unsuspecting people could trip over it in the dark, but restrained herself. "I should introduce myself. I'm Sherry Seaton. From KopyKats."

"What a lovely name . . . *Chérie*." His voice caressed the word, twisting its pronunciation.

Chérie? She had taken high school French and knew what that meant. "It's *Sher*ry. Accent on the first syllable."

"Yes, of course . . . *Chérie*," he said, without altering his pronunciation in the slightest.

She started to correct him a second time, then decided she'd just have to live with the endearment.

"Won't you come in a little farther?" he inquired politely.

"How do I know you don't have more booby traps waiting for me?" she muttered.

"Booby traps? I'm afraid I am not familiar with this expression."

"Never mind, it's not important." She took a few cautious steps forward.

"A little farther still. There, that is good. There is a

couch on the wall to your right. Be careful of the table in front of it."

If there was a couch, she must be in the living room of a suite. With the thought, a dozen tiny muscles relaxed and she recognized how tense she had been, assuming she was entering the Frenchman's bedroom.

Ridiculous! At twenty-seven, with a failed marriage behind her, she was too adult to quail at the mere thought of being in a bedroom with a man. Even a man with a sexy baritone, an intriguing accent, and a body whose masculinity had made her tingle in response.

She took another hesitant step forward. "If you could give me your score for the Wednesday session, I'll be on my way."

"Impossible."

She stared into the blackness. "Why is it impossible?"

"Without a light of some kind, I could not be certain I had given you the right music."

"Don't you have a flashlight? Or a candle?" The minute the words were out, she knew how silly they sounded.

"No, I regret I have not." His tone was elaborately thoughtful. "Do you know, not one of my travel guides suggested bringing a flashlight or a candle to an American luxury hotel? A serious oversight—I shall write to the publishers and complain."

She gulped. "I think I just won the dumb-question contest. Sorry. But I really do have to go. Can't we at least try to find your score?"

"We could try." He sounded dubious. "But even if we should succeed, I doubt if you would care to walk down twenty-one flights in the dark. With the electricity off, the elevators will not run."

"You have a point," Sherry admitted. Was it pure imagination, or did he sound as if he were enjoying this

ridiculous situation? "What do you suggest we do now?"
she asked.

"Why not sit down and relax? If you will make yourself comfortable, I promise I will not attack you." He
paused, then added, "I assure you it has been weeks,
months perhaps, since I last attacked a woman."

He probably hadn't had to, Sherry thought wryly. With
his self-assurance and the impression of solid, muscular
masculinity she had tasted during that one brief moment
in his arms, he probably had women falling over him in
droves.

Of course, for all she knew, he had the face of a
gargoyle . . . but if her glimpse of flashing black eyes and
a deep tan were anything to go by, he was about as far
from a gargoyle as anyone could get.

"Chérie? Are you still there?" He had stepped closer;
she could tell by the source of his voice and the faint
scent of an unfamiliar, musky after-shave.

"Of course I'm still here. You've made it all too clear
I can't go anywhere." She took a small sideways step
and her heel struck something that teetered alarmingly.
She reached down to steady the object; her fingers identified it as a rectangular leather case with a handle on
top. "More booby traps. I might have known," she muttered.

"I beg your pardon?"

"Nothing. I just ran into something. Some kind of
case, I think." She peered vainly into the darkness. "I
don't suppose it has your score in it?"

"Let me see . . ." His fingers brushed hers as he groped
for the case, and she drew back as a warm tingle spread
up her arm. "No, what you have found is a traveling bar
case, a gift from JRA. Would you care for a drink?"

"Oh, for heaven's sake!" Her frustration burst out of

control. "Here we are, stuck with no lights, I've got a job with an impossible deadline waiting for me, and you act as though this were a normal social occasion."

"But we *are* stuck here, Chérie. Nothing you or I can do will change that." His voice, calm and reasonable, made her feel like a child having a temper tantrum. "Why should we not enjoy ourselves as much as possible?"

"I suppose you're right," she said dubiously.

"I am. You will see. First, I suggest you take off your coat." He must have moved around behind her, for he touched the shoulders of her still-damp raincoat. His hands lingered near the back of her neck before he pulled the coat down her arms, and a surge of warmth took her by surprise.

The sudden onset of sensuality left her feeling scattered, as if her wits had turned to confetti and blown away.

"Let me guide you to the couch." His fingers closed on her upper arm and he urged her forward. One step. Then another, his hand snug on her arm, his body only inches from hers. Somehow, he seemed to be more vividly present in her mind than if she had been able to see him. His scent, an indefinable masculine odor combined with a musky after-shave, filled her nostrils and wafted upward to her brain. The warmth of his body was a palpable touch on the skin of her cheeks and throat, and she felt as if she could perceive the individual whorls and ridges of his fingertips on the bare skin above her elbow.

She sank onto a couch, her senses still hyperacute. The rain enclosed the room in a curtain of sound; the nubby fabric of the couch was a rough caress.

"Do you want a drink?" He had moved across the

room; she could tell by the now more distant placement of his voice.

"No, thank you," she said automatically, then reconsidered. "Oh, well, all right. I don't suppose one could hurt. What have you got?"

"One moment, let me find out." He paused. "My nose tells me this is bourbon. And here is scotch. Will one of those do?"

"Scotch will be fine. With water, if that's possible."

"Certainly it's possible."

Sounds told her he was pouring and mixing; the tinkle of ice cubes informed her the room had a refrigerator. At least his bartending kept him at a reasonable distance. Without his presence impinging on her senses, she was able to consider her predicament properly. The delay in getting to work was bad enough, but what if the lights stayed off and she was locked up with the crazy Frenchman for hours?

"Send for the men with the straitjackets," she murmured.

From across the room, he spoke. "Pardon? I'm afraid I did not hear you."

"It was nothing." She paused, then said to the darkness, "I should try to call my partner. She'll be wondering what's happened to me."

"Ah, yes, I see." She heard the sound of the receiver being lifted, then replaced. Regretfully, he said, "I am afraid the phone is also not working."

Biting her lower lip, she subsided back into the couch. She was only aware of his return when a glass clunked onto the table in front of her. A moment later, the cushions dipped as he lowered himself beside her.

She groped for her glass and sipped an excellent smoky

scotch. "Are you sure there's no way I can get out of here?"

"Chérie, Chérie," he said sadly. "You know there is nothing to be done about the situation. Why not relax and enjoy it?"

A part of her recognized how easy it would be to obey his suggestion and sink into lassitude. In the dark, his voice was hypnotic, a deep, seductive counterpoint to the steady rushing of the rain and the now-distant rumble of thunder.

She pulled herself up short. Relax? When there was an impossible deadline to be met?

His voice came, deep and soft, out of the darkness. "I do not wish to embarrass you, Chérie, but my curiousity is aroused. Why did you repeatedly hang up on me today?"

She gulped too big a mouthful of her drink and sputtered, "Oh, that!"

"Yes, that. Tell me . . ."

She exhaled a brief sigh. "You see, my partner and I have been getting a lot of obscene phone calls lately. So I assumed . . ."

"You thought I was an obscene caller?" He sounded incredulous.

"Yes, I'm afraid so. I'm sorry."

"No matter." As he spoke, he shifted slightly; his arm brushed hers and she retreated with the recognition of firmly defined muscles. Another spurt of warmth spread through her.

"I am sorry. I suppose I shouldn't have hung up on you." She tried to hold it in, then blurted, "It was partly your own fault, you know."

"Ah, yes. My misplaced sense of humor was responsible."

"Yes, that and..." She hesitated. "Why did you ask me to repeat your name?"

The wait before he spoke seemed endless, filled with the sound of his breathing and her own. When he spoke, it was so softly she had to lean closer to hear him. "Because your voice is so beautiful. A beautiful voice belonging to a beautiful woman."

Beautiful was something Sherry knew she wasn't. Of medium height and with average feminine curves, she had the most common of hair colorings—brown, though with the advantage that her hair was thick and soft with a tendency to curl at the ends.

Her facial structure she judged sadly undramatic. No knife-blade cheekbones for her, but a pleasant oval shape with a softly rounded chin. Her eyes were all right, green-flecked hazel with thick sable-brown lashes. But her nose was too short for distinction and her mouth too wide, the lower lip too full to allow her pretensions to an aristocratic hauteur.

She was nice-looking, maybe. Even pretty, when she worked at it. But not beautiful.

Yet, hearing his deep silky voice pronounce her so, she felt a thrill of pleasure...and instantly recognized an enormous fly buzzing around in the ointment—the fact that he could have had no better look at her than she at him.

Tartly, she said, "It's a nice line, but it won't work. For all you know, I have crossed eyes and buck teeth."

"Do you? Let me find out?"

Before she was aware of his movement, she felt his touch on her temple and jerked away. "Don't."

"But how else am I to discover the truth about the buck teeth?"

His hand found her hairline again, and she had an

irrational, indefensible urge to rest her head against his palm. Quashing it ruthlessly, she protested, "This is ridiculous."

"Why is it ridiculous? We are in the dark. We are strangers and we cannot see each other, except by touch."

When he put it that way, it almost sounded logical. "Well . . ." she equivocated.

"I know," he continued confidently. "First you 'see' me with your fingers. Then I will 'see' you. I will be candid, Chérie. I am taking a big chance you will discover the glass eye and the hideous scar."

Surprised by his nonsense, a laugh bubbled out of her. What was the harm in his suggestion? "I suppose it's all right," she said slowly.

"Come, I will guide you."

She let him capture her hand and direct it to his face. Focusing all her concentration in her fingertips, she began at his hairline and found his hair was thick and springy. She moved down his forehead to eyebrows that cut an oblique line, slanting upward from the bridge of his nose. Next were his eyes, the sparkling black eyes she had seen an instant before the lights went out. With feathery delicacy, she touched his closed eyelids, her fingers brushing thick, short lashes.

She shivered. She had found the fatal flaw in Jean-Claude's plan. This "seeing" was intimate and unexpectedly sensual. It was plain, old-fashioned touching, and the lavalike flow of heat deep within her body was testimony to its lack of innocence.

"No hideous scar, after all." She kept her tone light, hoping to dissipate the electric tension forming between them in the velvety blackness.

He said nothing, his silence somehow charged with meaning.

She had to stop touching him and stop it now. But if she lifted her hands from his face with her survey incomplete, he would guess what he was doing to her.

She bit her lip, her hands unmoving on his temples. She would finish as briskly and impersonally as possible, then make some excuse to keep him from exploring her in turn.

Lightly and quickly, she ran her fingers over the sides of his face, noting the acute angle of his cheekbones. Now his mouth. Praying he would not notice the faint tremor that had developed in her hands, she touched the clean arched bow of his upper lip, then his lower lip, full but firm.

"That's that, then," she said brightly, and lifted her hands from his face.

With a lightning grab, he seized her wrist and drew her hand back to his mouth. His lips, then the tip of his tongue, touched her lifeline, and a wave of sensation flooded through her . . . painfully sweet and infinitely pleasurable.

His breath caressing her palm, he murmured, "Chérie."

The hand circling her wrist pulled her toward him. Her thigh touched his and she felt rather than saw him move closer. He was going to kiss her. Heaven help her, she *wanted* him to kiss her. Her lips parted on a sigh.

Then a blinding light struck her eyes and she stared dazedly into Jean-Claude's face.

Chapter 2

THE GLARE OF the electric lights snapped Sherry back to her senses. Was she losing her mind? A moment before, she had been about to be kissed by a perfect stranger— with her full cooperation.

Then she looked at Jean-Claude and discovered she did not feel as if he were a stranger. Her fingers recognized the arch of his cheekbones, the broad, smooth forehead, the sensual curve of his lower lip. His hair had the thick, crisp texture her hands had sensed, springing in vigorous waves from his forehead.

Only his eyes surprised her; they were not black as she had thought, but a deep dark brown, the color of bittersweet chocolate. But the wicked laughter in them was exactly what she expected.

She was staring, she realized, and had been ever since the lights flicked on. Worse, her hand was still clasped in Jean-Claude's. She pulled it away and had to fight an impulse to rub one palm against the other to erase the lingering thrill of his kiss.

She stood and took several steps. As she had deduced,

they were in the living room of a suite. Easy chairs upholstered in beige and royal blue flanked the couch.

Turning to face Jean-Claude, she found him sitting erect on the edge of the couch. He was watching her, his dark eyes filled with amused awareness.

Embarrassed, she blurted, "Well, that was an interesting experience, wasn't it? Being in the dark, I mean?"

In a deep, meaningful voice, he replied, "You are right. I found the experience a most interesting one."

She was pretty sure he didn't mean the same thing she did, but she wasn't about to ask for clarification. "You'll be able to find your score now," she said pointedly.

"True." He pushed himself up from the yielding cushions and stood, very straight and tall. He was casually dressed in tan slacks and a pale blue shirt. Its open collar bared a strong, tanned throat, and the sleeves were rolled to the elbows, displaying muscular brown forearms. His shoulders and chest were as broad, and his waist as trim as she had deduced from that one heady moment in his arms.

"I had heard about American efficiency." He spoke in a musing undertone. "But I never thought I should find it regrettable."

"I beg your pardon?"

"The lights. It was very efficient of someone to get them back on so quickly."

"It seemed like a long time to me," Sherry retorted.

"Did it?" He slanted her a curious glance. "It did not seem long to me. Not long enough . . ." His dark-brown eyes traveled over her slender figure, lingering at the points where the red ribbed top and navy slacks outlined her graceful curves.

His survey complete, he smiled, a dazzling, brilliant

smile that took possession of his entire face. His lips curved upward at the corners; his eyes sparkled with good humor; in one cheek was a curving indentation not quite deep enough to be labeled a dimple.

It was a charming smile, an enchanting smile. For no apparent reason, Sherry felt an answering tug at the corners of her lips. A sense of *déjà vu* slipped over her, like the moving shadow of a wind-driven cloud. It was just such a smile that had delivered her—wrapped up in a neat little package of helpless infatuation—into the arms of Mark Rollinson, her former husband. Although, if anything, Jean-Claude's smile had ten times the voltage of Mark's.

The comparison drifted away as Jean-Claude said, "You look just as I thought you would, Chérie. Beautiful." He took a step toward her. "Stay a little longer. I can have dinner sent up. Let us continue to get to know each other."

For one insane moment, she was tempted to accept. Why not? She was hungry; she would have to eat sometime; another hour's delay wouldn't matter much...

Reason returned like the clap of a thunderbolt. She gave herself a mental shake and said, "It's kind of you to invite me, but I couldn't possibly stay. My partner is waiting for me, remember? We have to get started on your score."

His brows lifted and Sherry's fingers remembered their fine texture and the smooth roughness of his cheeks and chin. "Will another hour really make so much difference?"

"Every second counts." When had she developed a penchant for aphorisms? Next, she'd probably tell him, "A stitch in time saves nine," or "A penny saved is a penny earned." "Sorry," she added quickly. "I didn't mean to sound stuffy. It's just that the deadline really is tight."

He lifted his hand in a gesture that managed to combine entreaty and regret. "There is nothing I can do to change your mind?"

She shook her head. "Nothing."

He gave a reluctant sigh. "How I wish I had written only a little music for Wednesday instead of such a lot!"

"Frankly, I wish you had, too." But not for the same reasons as Jean-Claude's, she thought. Even with hours to spare, having dinner in his hotel room would have been a bad idea. Just look what had almost happened during their brief time together in the dark. "If I could have your score..."

He crossed the room to a table near the drapery-shrouded windows and from a six-inch pile of yellow manuscript paper extracted a section. "There. This is what you need."

Sherry met him halfway across the room and took the pages from him. Instantly, her professional instincts took charge, and she leafed through the music. As she absorbed the blackness of the notation, her stomach knotted. Every page was thick with penciled notes. There were thousands, each and every one of which had to be neatly inscribed on paper by exactly—she glanced at her watch—thirty-nine hours from now.

"Oh, brother," she muttered under her breath.

"Is something wrong? Is it difficult to read?"

She glanced at the top page. "No, on the contrary, it's a hundred times neater than most scores we get. Reading it won't be a problem. It's just that there's an awful lot of it."

"It is that kind of movie." His voice chimed an apologetic note. "The music must be big, thick, lush..."

"I wasn't criticizing, Jean-Claude. I was just thinking like a copyist."

"I understand."

"Now, I really have to go." She grabbed her raincoat from a chair and started for the door.

"Wait." She broke stride and looked inquiringly over her shoulder. "When will I see you again, Chérie?"

His question flustered her. Was he asking her for a date? Or was his inquiry a professional one, composer to copyist?

"I'm not sure," she equivocated. "I might be at the recording session Wednesday morning. My partner and I always flip a coin to decide which one of us goes."

"Then I shall hope very much for your victory."

Sherry cleared her throat and said gently, "Actually, when we've been copying all night, it's the person who *loses* who has to go to the session."

His eyes lingered on her face as if he were committing her features to memory. Then he shrugged, with his hands splayed outward. "I am sorry, Chérie, but in that case, I cannot help but hope for your defeat."

"What's he like?" Maggie asked curiously.

"Who? Jean-Claude?" Sherry extracted the second sheet of the composer's score from the photocopy machine. The first step on a job was to make duplicates so Sherry, Maggie and each of their assistants could work from a separate copy of the music.

"Oho! First names already. That sounds promising. Come on, tell me about him. Old, young?" Maggie prompted. "Fat, thin? Dark, fair?"

Sherry put the next yellow sheet on the glass and closed the lid. "Let's see. Age . . . early thirties, I think. Height, a little under six feet."

"Mm. Sounds perfect so far. Go on."

"He's certainly not fat." Sherry pressed the button to start the machine. "But he's not too thin either."

"Better and better. What else?"

Sherry shrugged. "I don't know. He has dark hair." And wicked chocolate eyes. And the touch of his mouth on her palm had made electric currents race through her body.

But she wasn't about to tell Maggie all of that. Her partner would only make a big deal out of it. Already, Maggie was too inclined to berate Sherry for her lack of interest in the men she'd met since her divorce.

"Let's get to the nitty-gritty," Maggie said. "Is he married?"

Sherry blinked, startled. "You know, Maggie, I haven't the faintest idea." She had assumed Jean-Claude had no permanent ties, but for all she knew, there was a wife and seven little Delacroix back in France. Come to think of it, wife or no, France was most likely where he'd go the minute *Guns and Roses* was finished.

A two-week relationship with a possibly married man. Perfect! she thought sarcastically.

"Can't you even guess whether he's married or not?" asked inquisitor Maggie.

"Shucks." Sherry snapped her fingers. "I knew I should have taken my crystal ball along."

"But you can usually get a pretty good idea from the way a guy acts," Maggie protested.

And that—how Jean-Claude had behaved—was best left undiscussed, Sherry thought.

Fortunately, at that moment the photocopy machine stopped humming, and Sherry gathered the long white sheets from the tray. "Okay, partner. Time to start cranking out the notes."

Laden with scores, they walked briskly toward the long table at the back where the four assistant copyists waited, pens filled and rulers ready to begin.

"What time is it?" Maggie asked.

Sherry looked up from the violin part she was struggling with and focused on the wall-clock behind Maggie's head. "Three-thirty."

Three-thirty, Wednesday morning. They had copied until late the night before, then had grabbed a few hours sleep before returning to the office. Since then, they had worked for fifteen hours without a break.

"How are you doing?"

Sherry sighed and rotated her shoulders, trying to relieve the cramp that was the inevitable penalty for so many hours in one position. "My muscles have gone to sleep. I only wish I could join them."

"Three-thirty blues," Maggie said wisely. "By four, you'll feel better."

The hours passed to the scrape of pens and the subdued murmur of the coffeepot. Much later, Maggie again looked up from her work. "Time?" she murmured vaguely.

Sherry glanced up at the clock. "Seven-twenty."

"Are we going to make it?"

Sherry looked over at the pile of pages, taller now, on the end of the table. "Just barely." Regretfully, she added, "There's no time to check any of it, though. And, I'm worried about the stuff Katya did."

Their newest assistant had come down with the flu during the night. Sherry had sent her home, resolving to double-check every page of Katya's work. But now there was no time.

At eight A.M., the monster spit out the last of the duplicated parts as the assistant copyists shrugged into

their coats and left the office. Sherry stacked the music
in order and packed it into a black fiber case stickered
with the KopyKats logo—a black cat with a quill pen
in its paw. When she had finished, she announced, "Coin-
flipping time."

Maggie had her feet propped up on her desk as she
massaged the back of her own neck. With the air of one
propounding a brilliant innovation, she exclaimed, "I was
just thinking, Sherry! Don't you think you ought to handle this one? After all, you've had all the contact with
Jean-Claude and the guy from JRA."

Sherry shook her head with slow vehemence. "Oh,
no, you don't. You just want to go home and sleep while
I'm slaving. Here." She held out a quarter. "Flip."

With a show of reluctance, Maggie took the coin and
spun it into the air. "Okay, call it."

"Heads."

Maggie uncovered the coin and flashed an evil grin.
"Why, look at that! The coin agrees with me."

"Let me see." Sherry peered suspiciously into Maggie's palm. The coin lay unmistakably tails up. "Okay,
you win. But if you think I'm going to forgive you for
sleeping while I'm at the studio, think again."

"Actually," Maggie said with studied innocence, "I
wasn't planning to sleep *all* day. I thought I'd nap, fix
myself some pancakes, nap, read the newspaper, nap . . ."

"You'll pay for this," Sherry muttered as she carried
the music case to the back door. But despite her exhaustion, she was looking forward to hearing Jean-
Claude's music. And to seeing him again, said an un-
compromisingly honest little voice in her mind.

By eight-thirty, she was in the small lounge adjacent
to the giant recording room at JRA Studios. She unpacked
the black case and handed the parts to the studio librarian.

Then she poured herself a cup of coffee from the pot in the lounge and stepped into the main room where the musicians were assembling. In one corner, a trumpet player blew long tones into his instrument. Here and there, other musicians noodled softly into their flutes or clarinets.

Her gaze was focused on the back of the room, where the percussionists were unpacking their exotic-looking instruments, so she did not notice Jean-Claude until he was only a few feet away.

"Chérie," he said softly. "Good morning." His eyes swept over her approvingly.

Oh, help! she thought. After all those hours of copying, she must look like one of those people drained of their life forces in a B-grade horror movie.

He, on the other hand, was alert and bursting with energy, trim and neat, though casual, in a loose, khaki-colored shirt and fashionably pleated khaki pants.

She smoothed her wrinkled tan wool skirt over her hips. "Good morning, Jean-Claude."

"I am delighted to see I won the flip of the coin," he announced.

Deciding to play along, she corrected him. "You didn't win. My partner did." She pulled a mournful face. "She's at home, sleeping."

A smile tiptoed through his eyes. "Ah, no, Chérie. Indisputably, I am the winner." Leaning closer, he confided, "I could have told you it would turn out this way. I have always been a lucky man."

Was he also a married man? she wondered. He wore no ring, but that didn't have to mean much. Married or unmarried, he was certainly an accomplished flirt.

He peered more closely at her face, and a frown creased his brow. "But I see now you are exhausted. You should not be here after all, Chérie."

"It's that bad, is it?" She wrinkled her nose at him.

"No, no, Chérie. You look lovely. I only meant..."

She rested her hand on his forearm. This time she was prepared for the little jolt she got from touching him, but its intensity surprised her. A sizzling current seemed to connect them.

Her mouth had dried up and she had to swallow in order to say, "It's all right, Jean-Claude. I understand what you meant. And I'm really okay."

"Jean-Claude." A big, burly man with a silk shirt open halfway to his navel clapped his hand onto Jean-Claude's shoulder. "I need to talk to you. The producers want some changes made and—"

"Have you met Chérie Seaton?" Jean-Claude interrupted. "Chérie, this is Andrew Watson."

"Oh, right," said the big man dismissively. "From KopyKats."

Sherry nodded and extended her hand. "Hello, Mr. Watson."

"Andy," he said automatically. Ignoring Sherry's outstretched hand, he turned to Jean-Claude. "Now, about those changes..." He began to describe a scene in detail.

She opened her mouth, planning to warn both men the parts had not been double-checked for errors, then closed it again, recognizing that Andrew Watson's verbal flow made interrupting impossible.

Murmuring an unnoticed "Excuse me," she retreated to the lounge to ponder the unsettling effect Jean-Claude had on her. He was really something else, she thought. Bright, amusing, charming...

Charming. Ice water trickled slowly through her veins.

Charming. If ever a man was exactly that, it was Jean-Claude Delacroix. Oh, Lord, was she doing it again?

She had always been a sucker for charm . . . charisma . . . whatever you called it. Both her father and her ex-husband possessed that quality in abundance. And it had blinded her to the lack in both men of the more solid traits of character.

That was three strikes against Jean-Claude. Possibly married. Almost certain to leave L.A. before long. And now she had identified him as the kind of man she ought to treat as if she were a recovering alcoholic offered a shot of straight Kentucky mash.

Three strikes and he's out, she thought determinedly. If she'd been in any danger of floating with the strong tide pulling her into Jean-Claude's uncharted seas, now was the time to swim for shore.

At the stroke of nine, Jean-Claude stepped up onto the podium at the front of the recording room and thumbed through the score pages on his music stand. Sherry propped open the glass door of the lounge to listen. It was still all right to be interested in his music, she decided. It didn't mean she had to fall for the man.

"Good morning, ladies and gentlemen." He glanced around the room, including the entire orchestra in his smile. "I would like to begin with Cue Twenty-three."

Twenty-three was one she remembered copying during the long night. A blurred wash of musical color, it was one of the easiest sections to perform.

Clever Jean-Claude to start with that one, she thought with admiration. By the time it had been recorded, the musicians would be warmed up and ready for the more difficult portions of the score.

His baton descended, weaving through the air in clean, clear arcs, and Sherry's admiration—purely professional, she assured herself—jumped another several notches. His music was wonderful, a delicate blending of woodwind and string colors subtly different from anything she had ever heard before.

She could go on listening forever, she thought after a while. If only she weren't so tired . . .

She left her station near the lounge door and sank onto the Naugahyde couch. Though she tried to keep listening, her eyelids felt so heavy she decided to let them close, just for a moment. A wisp of sound from the flute was the last thing she heard . . .

Until a horrible discord jerked her out of a pleasantly hazy dream. Instantly awake, she jumped to her feet to see Jean-Claude stop the orchestra with a downward slash of his baton.

"Is there a problem?" he asked of a clarinet player seated near the center of the orchestra.

The young man grimaced. "I'm sorry. I think my part must be wrong."

"Let me take a look." Jean-Claude jumped down from his podium and threaded his way through the orchestra to the clarinetist.

Sherry's heart lurched into overdrive. The clarinet parts had been copied by Katya, whose work she vowed to check . . . but hadn't.

Gritting her teeth, she stepped into the recording room just as Jean-Claude looked up from the clarinetist's music. His eyes met hers and he gave a tiny shake of his head.

She understood at once—the part was wrong. Squaring her shoulders for courage, she met Jean-Claude at the podium. With the clarinetist's folder in his hand, he pitched his voice for her ears alone. "We have a problem. At least four of the clarinet parts are mistransposed."

"Oh, brother!" She explained about Katya's illness, then let out an unhappy sigh. "But that's not really any excuse. I should have checked the parts." ·

Jean-Claude shook his head gently. "In the time you had, you could not do everything. In fact, it was a miracle you finished at all."

"It's still my fault for not checking," she insisted.

"You must stop taking all the responsibility onto your shoulders." He lowered his voice to a husky murmur. "Very lovely shoulders they are, too, Chérie."

She stared at him, amazed. How could he flirt when, by rights, he ought to be furious? Occasional errors in notes were excused in a rushed copying job. But that an entire part should be wrong was indefensible.

Jean-Claude's eyes left the shoulders he had praised to linger on her breasts, where her soft yellow sweater clung, outlining her curves. "Very lovely everything, Chérie."

She felt a faint wash of heat rising in her face and inside, too, as if all kinds of things were melting. Then she abruptly recalled where she was and glanced around to see if anyone was observing the byplay. But the musicians were engrossed in chatting among themselves. In a room holding nearly ninety people, it was as if she and Jean-Claude were alone, enclosed by a dome of intimacy.

Jean-Claude was responsible, she decided; it was the way he focused his entire being on her, as if the rest of the universe had ceased to exist. Lord, the man was magnetic!

Three strikes, Sherry. Remember?

She drew herself a fraction away from him. "I'm afraid we'd better check the other parts Katya copied. There could be more problems."

He nodded. "I will check. You go ahead and begin work."

Presently, he joined her in the lounge, where she had

hastily unpacked pens and extra music paper from her briefcase. "More?" she asked when she saw the frown hovering between his slanted brows.

"I fear so, Chérie. There are errors in both trumpet parts."

Sherry let out a groan. "Oh, Lord, what a mess! I'm so sorry, Jean-Claude."

A reassuring smile smoothed away his frown. "No more apologies, if you please. The only question is if you can correct the parts in time."

"I'll do it." She spoke with more confidence than she felt.

"Good. I will go on with the music that is correct." He stepped to her side. Briefly, he rested his hand on her shoulder, the warmth of his palm penetrating her fuzzy sweater. "Don't worry, Chérie. It will be all right."

The next two and a half hours seemed like weeks as Sherry fought to keep her cramped fingers moving across page after page of music. Her back ached and her eyes felt as if they were about to drop out of her head. But she couldn't even pause to shake out her stiffened muscles. Though she worked at top speed, each cue she finished was immediately snatched up by the librarian and taken to the appropriate instrumentalist.

As time wore on, she began to view the lunch hour as an oasis in mid-Sahara. That one hour with no recording being done was her chance to catch up—and possibly even finish redoing the botched parts.

At last the hour came. The orchestra broke and musicians in groups of twos and threes strolled past the glass door of the lounge. Sherry raised her arms above her head for a much-needed stretch. She squeezed her eyes shut and opened them to find Andrew Watson's bulk filling the doorway.

"I just heard what happened," he brayed. "Do you realize this kind of foul-up could cost a fortune?"

"I'm sorry, Mr. Watson," she said evenly. "One of our copyists fell ill last night while she was working. I'm afraid she wasn't as accurate as our people usually are."

He strode up to her improvised copying table, his broad face contorted in a ferocious scowl. "If we have to go overtime because of your firm's mistake, I'll personally see KopyKats never works again in this town."

Dismay bloomed in her like an evil plant. Andrew Watson was capable of carrying out his threat, she was certain. He had the power and, judging from the malignant expression on his face, would not hesitate to use it.

She struggled to sound confident. "You don't have anything to worry about. I'm positive I can finish correcting the problems in time."

"I sure as hell hope so." He shook a finger at her. "I'm warning you, you'd better not submit a bill for the extra—"

"Enough, Watson!" From the doorway, Jean-Claude's voice cut the air like a whipstroke. "There is no call to threaten Miss Seaton. She and her firm had an impossible deadline to meet." His eyes shot sparks at Andrew Watson, who seemed to shrink inside his silk shirt. "Need I point out the deadline was caused, in the first place, by your office's inefficiency?"

Andrew Watson's voice took on a placatory whine. "I suppose you have a point, Jean-Claude."

"In fact," Jean-Claude said sternly, "I believe JRA owes KopyKats a bonus."

Watson's chest expanded like an accordion. "A bonus! Now, that's going too far."

"Is it?" He advanced toward Watson, his mouth curved

in a grim smile. "Does anyone outside your office know about the failure to hire a copyist until two days—two days!—before the recording session?" Watson seemed to shrink again, but Jean-Claude went inexorably on, "What about the fact that I myself was given the wrong date to arrive in Los Angeles? Would the heads of JRA be interested in some of this information, do you suppose?"

The music supervisor made one last attempt to bluster. "You can't do that, Jean-Claude. That would be . . ."

"Blackmail," Jean-Claude smoothly supplied. "Yes, it would. But that does not mean I would hesitate to do it." He arched one dark eyebrow. "Well?"

Watson glanced uncertainly from Jean-Claude to Sherry and back again. "Well, I suppose. I . . . I didn't realize you were personally concerned with Ms. Seaton."

Jean-Claude stalked around the table. Standing behind Sherry, he rested his hand on her shoulder. "I choose to think you mean no insult to Miss Seaton with that remark."

"No, no. Of course not." Watson seemed almost to be dancing in his attempt to mollify Jean-Claude. "I didn't mean to say . . . That is . . ."

"About that bonus?" Jean-Claude spoke sharply.

"Sure, sure, Jean-Claude. Anything you say." He glanced at Sherry. "Sorry, Ms. Seaton. I guess I . . . I'll leave you to get on with your work." He slunk from the room.

Jean-Claude's hand still rested on her shoulder. "I'm sorry you were subjected to that unpleasantness. The man is an imbecile."

"That's all right," Sherry said slowly. Her eyes brightened as she looked up at Jean-Claude. Having a man leap to her defense was rather nice, she had discovered. No wonder medieval ladies got themselves in such awful jams—for the pure pleasure of having a knight on a white horse gallop to the rescue.

Smiling her gratitude, she said, "I really appreciate your defending me that way. But . . ." Her brow creased and she blurted, "Why did you do it? When you come right down to it, the errors were KopyKats' fault."

"Because you did not deserve to be threatened," he said promptly, then paused with an enigmatic smile hovering around his lips. "And for reasons of my own, perhaps."

She had a hunch she would be wise not to ask what those reasons were, so she only said, "Well, in any case, thank you."

"It was nothing." He narrowed his eyes and zeroed in on her tired features. *"Mon Dieu!* You are exhausted. Must you work alone? Couldn't your partner come and help?"

She shook her head. "I tried calling Maggie, but she wasn't in. Don't worry. I'll be all right." But she couldn't keep a sigh from her voice.

"No, you are not all right. Go home, Chérie."

"I can't," she protested. "I have to finish redoing the parts."

"How much is left to do?" He leaned over her shoulder as she showed him the remaining pages. "Yes, I see."

Slipping his hands under her arms, he gently lifted her upward to a standing position. As his fingers grazed the side of her breast, a ripple of sensation penetrated her fatigue.

"What are you doing?" She slid out of his grasp, but the sensation lingered, as if his touch had left a shadow on her skin.

"I am sending you home. With so little left to do, I can easily finish the parts before the lunch break is over."

Sherry stared at him incredulously. "You . . . copy?"

"Why not? In my student days, I often earned money for rent and food by copying music."

"But what about your lunch? I can't let you do it."

He closed her briefcase and put it into her hand. "You have no choice. I am your boss on this job, am I not?"

His encounter with Andrew Watson had made it perfectly clear who had the real power here. Sherry admitted, "Yes, I suppose you are."

He picked up her coat from the chair where she had left it, and draped it over her shoulders. "Your boss orders you to go home." A grin curved the corners of his lips. "You see, I want you to be well rested when I pick you up for dinner tonight."

"Dinner?" Everything seemed to be moving too fast. Jean-Claude had taken charge not only of Andrew Watson but of Sherry herself. And at bottom she didn't seem to mind, not as she would have minded had any other man started ordering her around.

"Dinner." Jean-Claude's tone was confident. "I will pick you up at eight o'clock."

Her shoulders slumped, and for the first time she allowed herself to feel the full weight of her fatigue. She didn't have a choice, she decided. After his defense of her, the least she could do was have dinner with him. She said with uncharacteristic meekness, "All right, Jean-Claude. Eight o'clock."

She crossed the room and left the lounge. But before the door closed behind her, she heard a soft, satisfied chuckle; Jean-Claude was laughing.

Chapter 3

SHERRY UNLOCKED THE apartment door, mentally debating the only question she was still awake enough to consider: bath first, then sleep, or sleep first?

But as she stepped into the living room, she let out a groan. Maggie must have started moving into Jake's apartment, for a box half filled with odds and ends sat in the middle of the russet-colored carpet. Thrown over the back of the flowered-chintz couch were half a dozen towels and a T-shirt. Strewn untidily across the walnut coffee table were a dozen of Maggie's favorite spy novels.

Tidying up was decidedly not on Sherry's list of priorities. Later, she thought. After she'd slept. If she set her clock radio for six-thirty, she'd have plenty of time to shower, dress, and make the apartment look presentable before Jean-Claude arrived.

On top of the cherrywood dresser in her neat blue-and-white bedroom was her guitar. She ran her hand lightly across the strings and winced at the out-of-tune discord hummed by the instrument. "I'll get back to you soon, I promise," she murmured, then had to chuckle at herself for talking to a guitar.

She must be punchy from too much copying . . . and from too big a dose of Jean-Claude? After chalking up three strikes against him and making a firm decision, here she was, committed to having dinner with him.

She was too tired to worry about it now, she decided. She slipped into a yellow flannel nightgown, then set the alarm. Almost as soon as her head hit the pillow, she fell into a heavy sleep.

A noise woke her, and she sat bolt upright to peer dazedly at her clock radio. The digital display read seven-thirty-two. What had happened? The alarm should have gone off at six-thirty.

She took a closer look and found she'd accidentally set it for six-thirty A.M., not P.M. Oh, brother! Now, she really had to hustle.

As she swung her legs over the side of the bed, she wondered what had woken her, since it hadn't been the alarm. As if answering her question, the doorbell pealed— for the second time, she suspected. It was still too early for Jean-Claude, thank heaven, so it had to be Maggie, who often forgot her key.

She slipped an aged terry-cloth robe over her nightgown and hurried to the door. "Maggie, is that you?" she called as she struggled with the lock.

"No, it is I, Jean-Claude."

She wrestled the door open, suddenly horrifyingly aware of her hair in wisps and tangles, her eyes puffy from sleep. "You . . . you're early," she blurted.

Dismay flooded his dark eyes. "I didn't want to call and awaken you. I decided you might be too tired to go

out for dinner." He gestured at his feet where three bulging shopping bags sat in a row. "So I brought dinner to
you."

Dinner was not all he had brought. In his hand were
the strings of a dozen, helium-filled balloons—red, blue,
and yellow circles bobbling over his head.

She choked, fought to stifle a laugh, then chortled,
"Balloons, Jean-Claude?"

"I hope you like them, Chérie."

"Oh, yes. I like balloons very much."

A dozen feet down the hall, a door opened. One of
Sherry's neighbors, a middle-aged widow, stared at them
open-mouthed.

"Hello, Mrs.—" Sherry began, then stopped as she
saw the half-curious, half-horrified expression on the
woman's face. And no wonder. Here was Sherry in her
bathrobe, her hair tangled from sleep, and on her doorstep
was a mad Frenchman holding a bouquet of balloons.

"I was just . . . We were . . ." She gave up trying to
explain and said simply, "Good evening, Mrs. White."

Twice, the woman tried and failed before producing
a stammered, "Good evening, Sherry." She walked down
the hall, her back expressing a mixture of curiosity and
shock.

Sherry's eyes met Jean-Claude's. His look of barely
controlled mirth set her off and she had to clamp both
hands over her mouth to stifle a new attack of the giggles.

Finally, she regained enough control to say, "You'd
better come in before Mrs. White calls the asylum to
report an escaped patient."

He pulled down the balloons so they cleared the top
of the doorway, and thrust the strings into Sherry's hand.

"What do you think I should do with them?" she

asked. "I can hardly put them in a vase."

"Why not let them go?"

"I believe I will." She uncurled her fingers and the bright spots of color floated to the ceiling, bobbing gently and bumping one another before settling into a sparse mosaic.

Then Sherry's glance fell on the disordered living room. *Drat!* She'd forgotten about the flotsam Maggie had left behind.

"As you can see, the place is a bit of a mess," she said. "My roommate's in the process of moving out."

What shape was the rest of the place in? she wondered. The last time they'd been in the apartment, Maggie had prepared a meal they'd elected to call breakfast, even though it was past midnight. In the kitchen, Jean-Claude was likely to find plates of congealed egg yolks, a frying pan full of rancid bacon fat, and who-knew-what other horrors.

She shuddered. "Let me just check the kitchen."

She took a step in that direction, then stopped dead. Compared to how she must look, the apartment was a vision of loveliness. "On the other hand, I suppose I ought to get dressed first. I must be a sight."

Jean-Claude's eyes touched her as he struggled inside with the groceries. "As a matter of fact, you look perfectly delightful."

"Gosh, I'm so glad you noticed," she said flippantly. "I got dressed up just for you."

A puzzled frown formed between his slanted brows. "You are truly not aware of your beauty, are you, Chérie?"

It was Sherry's turn to look puzzled. He couldn't be serious, not when she was un-made-up and wearing a wreck of a robe.

"If you'll excuse me," she said with a grin, "I think I'll slip into something a little less comfortable. I won't be a minute."

Around one bulging grocery bag, he said, "Please take your time, Chérie. I already feel bad about showing up on your doorstep ahead of schedule. Help relieve my guilt by doing whatever you would do if I were not here. I assure you I can find my way around the kitchen."

Sherry hesitated for a moment, then nodded. "All right. If you're sure you don't mind . . ."

In the bathroom, she peered into the mirror, searching for traces of the beauty Jean-Claude claimed to see in her. All she found was the same old Sherry Seaton, wearing not a smidgen of makeup and a faded, ripped bathrobe.

She groaned. Beautiful, indeed!

But in her face was something—a sparkle in the eyes, a curve of anticipation to the mouth—she hadn't seen in a long, long time.

She filled the bath and poured in a capful of scented bath oil. Do whatever you would do if I were not here, he had said. But when she lifted her nightgown over her head, she found it not so easy to ignore Jean-Claude's presence.

From the kitchen came the muted clatter of pots and pans. A deep baritone began singing, too softly for her to identify the words or even really hear the tune. But he was there. He was most definitely there.

She paused with one foot on the rim of the bathtub. With Jean-Claude only a thin wall away, she was vividly aware of her nakedness. A sense of excitement, of almost physical anticipation, had risen in her that had absolutely no business being there.

Remember the three strikes, Sherry, she thought. Jean-

Claude was out—out of the question.

As she climbed into her bath, she brooded. The last thing she wanted in her life was a charmer like Jean-Claude. What she needed was a nice reliable accountant. Or a dentist. Someone who'd come home right on time every night. Someone dependable and predictable who would never go dancing off, leaving her alone.

Surprised, she sat up straight, soapy water sluicing over her breasts. It was the first time since her divorce she had thought in terms of *needing* anyone at all.

But she could see from her reaction to Jean-Claude that something had changed. The idea of a man in her life was beginning to have a strong appeal. Not Jean-Claude, of course. Not if he turned out to be cast from the same mold as her father and her ex-husband, men with charm in abundance but with no depth, no solidity, no ability to make a commitment and live up to it.

Toweled dry, she brushed out her long hair so it fell in a bell curve around her shoulders, then dressed in a hostess gown she had bought on impulse and never worn. Its velvety skirt was dusty rose, the long-sleeved bodice a thin white knit. A pair of white sandals, gold hoop earrings, and her usual discreet makeup completed the look she wanted—relaxed but gracious, totally at ease, despite the presence of a devastatingly attractive man in her apartment.

Good luck, Sherry, she thought sarcastically as she whisked around the living room gathering up Maggie's debris. After hiding it in the coat closet, she walked to the open kitchen door to watch Jean-Claude at work.

He had tied a huge apron over his gray slacks and charcoal pullover. Whistling a simple tune, he cut paper-thin slices from a fresh green zucchini.

"You have quite a repertoire," Sherry commented from

the doorway. "Do you always hum or sing or whistle while you cook?"

He pivoted to face her. His sleeves were pushed up to his elbows, baring muscular forearms. An appealing tuft of dark hair curled over the V-neck of his sweater. His eyes widened. "You are breathtaking, Chérie."

She dipped a quick curtsy. "Thank you, kind sir."

His warm gaze lingered on her and she was suddenly aware of her breasts pushing against the thin knit bodice. She felt her nipples tightening and had to resist the impulse to hide them behind crossed arms.

At last, he said, "I must confess, I usually make some sort of music when I cook. I enjoy cooking. It makes me happy . . ." He flashed a quick grin, his teeth sparkling against his tanned face. "And when I am happy—*voilà!*— I sing. I hope I didn't disturb your bath."

"No, not a bit," Sherry lied, then added, "Can I do anything to help?"

He had erased any traces of disarray from the kitchen. The yellow counter tiles gleamed; the old wooden kitchen table looked freshly scrubbed.

"You might pour us each a glass of wine," he said.

"Wine . . . uh, I don't think we have any."

"I brought some. It's in the refrigerator." He faced her accusingly, his hands on his aproned hips. "And what a refrigerator! Two brown stalks of celery, a half-eaten container of yogurt, one egg, and half a strip of bacon. Don't you ever eat?"

Sherry crossed the room and opened the refrigerator door; the shelves now held enough to feed an army. Feeling as if she were confessing to a loathing of cuddly puppies and innocent children, she said, "I eat, all right. I just don't cook." She took a bottle of white wine and filled two goblets.

Seeming unfazed by her confession, Jean-Claude took the glass of wine she handed him. "Do you dislike cooking?" he inquired.

It wasn't that she disliked it, exactly, but that things burned or scorched or perversely came out raw whenever she was in charge. So she told him, "I have to admit, it's not my favorite thing."

"Then there is no reason you should cook." He smiled lazily, something in his eyes sending tingles up Sherry's spine. "However, since one must eat, it is fortunate that I enjoy cooking, is it not?"

What was he implying? That they might share many more meals, with Jean-Claude the chef? "I suppose that's convenient for you," she said equivocally. "What are you fixing, by the way?"

"A simple meal." His dark eyes sparkled with laughter. "Tureen of fresh vegetables, roast duck stuffed with corn bread and wild mushrooms, and an apricot soufflé."

"A simple meal?" Sherry groaned. "What are you, a refugee from a three-star restaurant?"

"In effect, yes."

The timbre of his voice made her say slowly, "You're serious, aren't you?"

"Perfectly serious. My family owns a restaurant in Paris."

She pulled up a chair and sat down, staring at him with frank amazement. "And I suppose it *is* a three-star restaurant!"

"The *Guide Michelin* has been kind enough to honor it with that rating."

She took a sip of the wine. "Since you're so fond of cooking, I'm surprised you didn't end up in the family business."

Jean-Claude smiled and started chopping something

green into tiny bits. "I tell you truthfully, Chérie, it was difficult to decide between being a professional chef with music as a hobby or a musician who cooks for pleasure. But at last I decided on the latter course for the simplest of reasons—it is difficult for an amateur composer to get his music performed, but not at all difficult for an amateur chef to find people willing to eat his creations."

Sherry laughed. "I see your point. But didn't your family mind?"

"A little at first, perhaps, because of the family tradition. But not so much, because my younger brother was eager to step into my shoes."

"You have a younger brother?"

"Three of them."

"Really?" She propped her elbows on the table and rested her chin on her laced fingers. "Tell me about your family, Jean-Claude."

He went back to his chopping. "It is not very interesting," he warned.

"I'm sure it is," Sherry said, meaning it. Nothing about Jean-Claude could be boring, she was certain.

He spun out a series of entertaining tales. Aunts and uncles. Cousins. Brothers and sisters. There seemed to be hundreds of Delacroix, a tight-knit clan whose frequent brawls were tempered by affection.

By the time she had finished her glass of wine, he had her laughing over a story about the aging duke who had courted his great-aunt Mireille for nearly forty years.

He deftly stripped the skin from an apricot and said, "There, that is done. Now we have only to wait."

Delicious smells pervaded the kitchen. Jean-Claude went to the refrigerator for the bottle of wine and refilled their glasses. As he pulled out the chair next to Sherry's, he said, "You have heard a great deal about my family.

What about your own? Are your parents still alive?"

"My father is." As far as she knew. It had been nearly a year since the last time Flying Bill had popped up. But there were all kinds of things to account for his absence. It would be months yet before she started to worry. "My mother died when I was born," she told Jean-Claude.

He cast her a quick sympathetic look, then picked up her hand and began toying idly with her fingers. "Did you have a lonely childhood, Chérie?"

She didn't want to sound like a poor little orphan girl. But what he was doing to her hand was distracting enough that she admitted, "I guess I did, a little. I was brought up mostly by an aunt. She did her best, but she was really too old and set in her ways to cope with a child."

"And your papa?"

As he waited for her answer, he turned her hand over and ran one finger across her palm. Sensation zinged through her and she couldn't think clearly enough to say anything except the truth. "He wasn't around much."

"I see." The look in his eyes said he saw more than was comfortable for her. She didn't want to confide in Jean-Claude. If she did, she would only find him more difficult to resist.

What he was doing to her hand was another problem. As he continued to draw designs on her palm, warmth spread up her arm and through her body. "Jean-Claude, stop! That tickles," she reproached him.

His eyebrows rose, but he loosened his grip enough that she was able to retrieve her hand, which she wrapped defensively around the stem of her wineglass.

He sipped his wine, then sat back in his chair. "What about your life since you grew up? You have not married?"

She threw him a quick sideways glance. "Actually, I

was married. We were divorced three years ago."

Now was the time to check out strike number one. The question formed on her tongue, but she pressed her lips firmly together. To ask would be to reveal that she was romantically interested in him.

Jean-Claude studied her face, and silent laughter blossomed in his eyes. "To answer your question—no. I have never married."

There went strike number one!

"I didn't ask," she protested.

His grin was infuriatingly smug. "But you wanted very much to inquire, did you not?"

"Of course not. It never even crossed my mind."

He let out a warm chuckle. "You prefer me to believe you make a habit of dining *en intime* with married men?"

Flustered, she spluttered, "No, no. Of course not." She cast about for a change of subject and said hastily, "Jean-Claude, about your music . . ." She described one of the subtle effects she had heard that morning. "How did you get that sound?"

He produced the facial equivalent of a shrug. "It was, in effect, a trick. One writes the piccolo in its lowest range, the clarinets in their highest. *Voilà!*"

She thought about that for a moment, then said with dawning comprehension, "Oh, I see how you did it."

His eyes lit with interest. "So! You are a trained musician."

Sherry nodded. "I was a music major in college. Most copyists are, you know."

"In what area of music were you trained?"

"I majored in composition, actually." She felt embarrassed admitting her background was similar to Jean-Claude's. Her current work seemed so mundane compared with his flights of creativity.

Curiosity sparked in his eyes. "So you are a composer, too! What kind of music are you writing now, Chérie?"

She glanced down at her wineglass. "I'm not composing at all anymore." What she did these days with her musical talent was something she had confided only to a few close friends. Probably it would sound silly to Jean-Claude.

"But that is a great pity!" he exclaimed. "When one has ability, one should use it."

"It's almost impossible to make a living as a composer," she pointed out.

"True. Unless one is fortunate, as I was, to find a career in films." He smiled, putting her at ease. "Tell me more, Chérie. Have you been a copyist ever since you left college?"

She shook her head, thinking back to the two years when she had supported both herself and Mark with a succession of menial jobs. "No, I did a lot of other things before Maggie and I started KopyKats."

He said carefully, "Copying is all very well for a time, but I would think a creative person would soon find it suffocating."

His criticism was too close for comfort to the thoughts that had recently plagued her. Hoping to convince herself as much as him, she said stoutly, "Copying is a highly skilled trade. It suits me just fine." Without thinking, she reached up and rubbed the muscles at the base of her neck, still sore from her long hours bent over a desk.

Jean-Claude looked closely at her. "You are stiff from copying." He leaped to his feet and moved around behind her chair. "Allow me."

Sweeping her hair to one side, he began to massage her shoulders. His touch was neither too gentle nor too rough, and some level of Sherry's senses responded instantly, as if every nerve in her body focused on the places his hands touched.

"I did not intend my comment as an insult to your profession, Chérie," he said gently. "I know how difficult and demanding the work can be."

She sighed, no longer even slightly defensive. "I have to admit it isn't always the most exciting job."

Jean-Claude continued to massage her back until, bit by bit, she relaxed. She couldn't be sure when it changed from an innocuous backrub to something else. A fluid warmth softened her body. Bones, muscles, tendons all seemed to dissolve, and the mental signs she had posted, warning her away from Jean-Claude, were blurring, getting fuzzy and meaningless.

She said dreamily, "You give a terrific backrub, Jean-Claude. It's awfully nice of you. That's the fourth nice thing you've done for me today." She paused, finding it difficult to think clearly with his hands moving on her shoulders. "Or is it the fifth? I'm afraid I've lost count."

His hands continued their rhythmic motions. "Pardon? I'm afraid I do not understand."

She ticked them off on rubbery fingers. "You defended me to Andrew Watson. Finished copying the parts. Brought me balloons and dinner. And now a backrub."

"It was nothing, Chérie." His voice sounded very deep and soft. If you will let me, this is only the beginning of things I would like to do for you . . . and for myself."

That arrowed through her haze . . . a remark she wouldn't touch with a pair of tongs, she thought. Time to change the subject again.

Pulling herself up straighter in her chair, she turned her head to look at him. "I've been meaning to ask you, how did the rest of the session go?"

"Very well. The musicians are excellent."

One of his hands left her neck. Slipping his palm along the side of her cheek, he gently pushed her head so she was again facing forward. His little finger grazed the corner of her mouth, and she had a momentary, insane desire to capture his fingertip with her lips. She sternly quelled the impulse and he returned his hand to her shoulder, but the sensations invading her body seemed to have trebled in intensity.

Somehow she had to make him stop without letting him find out how strongly he was affecting her. It was ridiculous, melting into little puddles merely because of a backrub.

A sneaky ploy occurred to her. She sniffed and asked innocently, "Do I smell something burning?"

Jean-Claude started and lifted his hands from her shoulders. *"Dieu!* I hope not!" Swiftly, he checked the oven and the pots on the burners. "Everything is fine. Only a moment more and we can eat."

Dinner, served on the old country table with candles glowing softly and a few of the balloons brought in from the living room for decoration, was the most delicious meal Sherry had ever eaten.

The conversation remained light; Sherry was only marginally aware of how skillfully Jean-Claude drew her out concerning her likes and dislikes, her habits and opinions.

When they were through eating, he stood and held out his hand. "Come, we will have our aperitif in the living room."

By now she was replete with good food and several glasses of wine. Settled onto the couch, she felt as if she might start purring from sheer contentment.

He brought her a small glass holding a mouthful of crème de menthe, then gestured toward her small but excellent stereo system. "May we have music?"

"That would be nice." Too languorous to make a decision, she suggested, "Why don't you choose something?"

In a moment, the sounds of one of her favorite records wafted through the room. "Britten folk songs." She named the record, a rendition of traditional English ballads by composer Benjamin Britten. "Are you a Britten fan?"

"Indeed. I studied with him for a while."

Her eyes widened with interest. "I'm impressed. Studying with him must have been wonderful."

Jean-Claude's long easy stride brought him to the couch. He sat down beside her and said, "Maestro Britten was an extraordinary man. Someday, if you like, I will tell you about him."

She flicked him a curious glance. "Why not tell me now?"

"Chérie, there are times to talk and times to be silent." He gave her a long, meaningful look; in his dark eyes was a soft golden glow. "Now, I think, is a time for silence."

Instantly, every nerve in Sherry's body was alert and trained on the powerful masculine body only inches from hers. Then, pulled by a force she did not understand, she lifted her eyes to look at Jean-Claude's face. As if in a dream, she watched him reach out, take her aperitif glass from her hand, and set it on the coffee table.

"I sense you are reluctant to let me touch you." He looked sad. "Why is that, Chérie?"

He had it wrong, she thought. She wasn't reluctant at all. If anything, she was much too eager for his touch, considering there were still two strikes against him. "We

... we don't know each other very well," she said nervously.

"We are learning about each other, are we not? We have talked. And we will talk more. But there are ways other than conversation for a man and a woman to learn about each other."

He reached out. One of his beautifully made, long-fingered hands touched her hair, lifting the fine tendrils that feathered around her temples. "For instance, I have just learned that your hair is like silk."

With a careful hand, he traced the line of her brow, then circled her eyesocket. "Now I am learning that your skin is softer than velvet."

She was too mesmerized to draw away. Her lashes fluttered, then brushed her cheeks as his hands played lightly on her face. His fingers touched her lips, which trembled as he traced their outline; then he trailed his hand down her chin to the side of her throat. "Chérie," he said in a soft, husky voice.

Sensations she had only dimly imagined stirred in a slow, languorous awakening as his hand circled the base of her throat, then slipped beneath her heavy hair to cup the back of her neck. He bent toward her and his mouth met hers.

At first it was the lightest of kisses, feather-soft. When she felt the tip of his tongue teasing at the corner of her mouth, she parted her lips with an exhalation of breath that turned into a sigh.

His tongue touched hers and she felt a rush of desire so acute it seemed as if her senses had been fueled and were waiting only for Jean-Claude to ignite them into full-flaming life.

The intensity of her reaction brought her up short. If she wanted a man, she ought to be out looking for that dentist. But there were no dentists in the room. There was only the intoxicating physical presence of Jean-Claude.

He wrapped his arms around her, then lifted his mouth from hers to stare deeply into her eyes. "Don't be afraid, Chérie," he said softly. "I would never hurt you."

All her warnings and cautions slipped away and it felt perfectly natural to be in Jean-Claude's arms. "I'm not afraid," she assured him.

"Good." The single syllable was husky with satisfaction and desire.

She was afloat in the deep, dark pools of his eyes. She could feel his breathing as if it were her own, her chest lifting and falling in rhythm with his, her heart beating against the soft fabric of his sweater in the same tempo as his heartbeat.

When he kissed her again, more deeply, exploring the moistness of her mouth, she fell into a swirling maelstrom of sensation. She was dizzy; she was drowning. Unless she reached out for support, she would be swept away and lost.

Involuntarily, she clutched his upper arms to steady herself. As her hands touched the rock-hard muscles, his kiss deepened. Her arms crept up around his neck and her fingers twined in the crisp softness of his hair.

Still exploring her mouth with his own, he shifted his position and cupped the weight of her breast in his palm. A moan of longing escaped her as her breast pushed against his seeking fingers, the nipple puckering into a marble peak. His thumb found the hardened tip and he exhaled a sigh of pleasure.

She was on fire and drowning, both at the same time. Hot and cold. Floating as lightly as one of Jean-Claude's balloons and heavy with the molten weight of earth.

He pulled her closer, though his hand continued its sweet torment of her breast, and the pressure of his thigh against hers fueled her pleasure and her need.

He groaned, "Chérie, my angel. I want to make love to you." Returning his mouth to hers, he kissed her with a deep and eloquent hunger.

In her ears, the thunder of desire blotted out all conscious thought. She wanted him ferociously. She needed him. Nothing else mattered.

Yes, Jean-Claude. Yes. The words beat in her brain and she broke from his kiss to speak them aloud. But there was a sound, an impossible, distracting sound, somewhere in the room. With eyes half-blinded by passion, Sherry looked up to see Maggie's rueful face framed in the doorway.

Chapter 4

FOR ONCE, MAGGIE was so abashed she stammered. "Oh, g-golly! I'm sorry." Behind her was Jake—big and broad, with the sun-streaked blond hair of an ardent though now overage surfer.

Sherry struggled out of Jean-Claude's embrace and stood, tugging down the rumpled skirt of her hostess gown. Her heart was tripping double-time, and she was certain the flush of desire must show on her throat. "That's all right," she said untruthfully, then managed to make introductions all around.

Maggie explained, "Jake and I just stopped by to pick up another load of my stuff. I should have called first, but I didn't think . . ." She bit her lip. "Oh, dear. Maybe we should just go."

"Don't be silly," Sherry said. "Go ahead and get your things. Jean-Claude was just about to leave, anyway."

His brows rose at that, but he said pleasantly, "I am not in such a hurry that I cannot assist in the moving operation."

And so they all scurried around under Maggie's direction, gathering things and piling them into boxes. While they worked, Sherry had time to reweave the tattered fabric of her common sense.

When she and Maggie ended up in the kitchen, the redhead announced with relish, "I only have one thing to say, partner, and that's—wow! He's gorgeous."

Sherry mumbled something noncommittal. Jean-Claude was gorgeous, all right. And his charm was as dangerous to her as an addictive drug. Not to mention that other strike still against him—the likelihood he would only be in L.A. for as long as it took to complete *Guns and Roses*.

"I'm sorry about bursting in like that," Maggie apologized.

"It's really all right," Sherry said sincerely. If anything, she owed Maggie and Jake a giant debt of gratitude for arriving when they did. Saved by a pair of unlikely bells, she thought.

"It won't happen again. In the future, I'll call before I drop by. I'll get the rest of my stuff tomorrow." Maggie's blue eyes twinkled. "Not too early tomorrow, I promise."

"I told you, Jean-Claude was just leaving," Sherry insisted.

"Sure," Maggie said knowingly.

After the redhead left the kitchen, Sherry piled a frying pan and Dutch oven into a box and packed dishtowels around them, but only a fraction of her mind was on her task.

She measured a quarter of an inch with thumb and forefinger; she had come *that* close to making love with Jean-Claude. Which would have meant, inevitably, getting all tangled up with another charmer who was bound to break her heart.

What made her a pushover for such men? She ought to be able to recognize the type from blocks away, since she had been exposed to one of them from birth—her father, Flying Bill Seaton. Though he had earned the label for other reasons, Flying Bill was the perfect name for him: His idea of parenting had been to make lightning visits twice a year. A few days of laughter, a few days when Sherry felt like the most special daughter in the universe, and off he would go, leaving loneliness behind him.

Sherry's ex-husband had been another charmer. A talented guitarist, Mark had disarmed her with his smile and his sense of humor. The trouble was that he gave no thought to the little things—like rent and food and clothing. When he wasn't working, he expected Sherry's waitressing job to support them both. When he was working, he was invariably on the road, and she suffered loneliness reminiscent of all those years of waiting for her father's visits.

Charming to the end, Mark managed to convince Sherry a divorce would be for her benefit. She felt both gratitude and guilt until, several months later, she learned of Mark's longtime liaison with a female backup singer.

Even so, his fidelity had never been the issue. The problem had been the vagaries of his work and—ultimately—his inability to make a real commitment.

In the wake of her divorce, she had vowed to become independent, both financially and emotionally, so nothing could ever again rock the foundations of her world. Next she had promised herself that if she ever fell in love again, it would be with someone solid and stable, a man who understood duty, responsibility, and commitment.

So what was she doing with Jean-Claude Delacroix? He was clearly the kind who danced through life, shooting off sparks and leaving behind a trail of singed hearts.

There should be a vaccination she could take, Sherry thought wryly. Something to inoculate her against that type of man. Or a pill—one in the morning and one at night and Jean-Claude's charm would roll off her like water from a duck's back. However, since she had no miracle medication in her bathroom cabinet, she would simply have to find the strength to resist him all on her own.

She finished packing the box of kitchen things and took it to the living room for one of the men to carry downstairs. With all four of them working, Jake's station wagon was soon full.

At the door of the apartment, Jake shook Jean-Claude's hand. "Thanks, man, for the help."

"Yes, thanks a bunch," Maggie chimed in. "See you tomorrow at the office, Sherry. Bye."

With uneasy formality, Sherry turned to Jean-Claude. "It was very nice of you to help."

"It was nothing." He dropped his hand lightly onto her shoulder, then slid his palm under her hair to warm the back of her neck. As if no time had elapsed since the last time he'd touched her, sensation sprouted and blossomed along her nerve endings.

"Shall we have more music?" he asked.

Sherry shook her head. "Thank you for the dinner. It was a wonderful meal. But it is getting awfully late."

"It is not that late, not even ten o'clock."

She took a backward step away from him, intending to escape the insidious warmth flowing from the touch of his hand. But he seemed to anticipate her retreat and fluidly followed her, his fingers remaining on the back of her neck.

"I have to get up early to start copying the next segment of your score," she pointed out.

Laughter rose in his eyes. "Then you are even more efficient than I thought."

"What are you talking about?"

He broke into a broad grin. "How are you to begin copying something that I have not yet given to you?"

Sherry gasped. "I forgot! I should have gotten the next section of your score from you at the studio today."

"No matter." His thumb moved on the silken skin of her throat in a persistent, will-destroying rhythm. "I will send it to you tomorrow morning by messenger."

"Oh, good. Thank you." She tried to blot out recognition of the tendrils of warmth curling through her.

"But I will not be sending the messenger until eleven or so. So you see, Chérie, there is no reason to send me away so early."

She stiffened, lifting her chin. "I still think you should go, Jean-Claude. In fact, I'm asking you to leave."

He disengaged his hand from her neck and dropped his arm to his side. With all the laughter gone from his face, he said, "Tell me honestly, Chérie. If your friends had not shown up when they did, would you have let me make love to you?"

She dropped her gaze to the russet carpet. "Maybe. I'm not really sure." Maybe? In a pig's eye! She had been a split-second from *asking* him to make love to her. "I might have said yes," she confessed, "but . . ." She paused, biting her lip.

"But?" he prompted gently.

Lifting her eyes to his face, she said in a rush, "But it would have been a mistake. I admit I got a little carried away. You're a very attractive man, Jean-Claude."

He placed both his hands on her waist, his fingers splaying out on her back. "And you, *ma chérie,* are a very beautiful woman. But there is more to it than that, *n'est-ce pas?* A current flowing between us, something special, something intense, from the very beginning."

One of his hands dropped lower, his thumb curving over her hipbone. Sherry wasn't certain whether he took a step toward her or whether he pulled her closer to him, but suddenly the distance between them was halved. His thigh was only a few inches from hers.

Defensively, she said "That's a nice line, Jean-Claude." He was full of them; the man had more lines than a marching band. "But after all, we hardly know each other."

"We know enough, I think. But I do see your point."

Again someone moved, though Sherry was certain it wasn't she and she hadn't detected Jean-Claude taking a step. It was black magic, she thought with a trace of hysteria. He must be a wizard.

She tried visualizing him in a tall coned hat and robes, but at that moment his thighs brushed hers, generating waves of fire that licked through her like the onset of a fever, and she could only see him as he was—handsome, virile, infinitely appealing.

"I can understand why you would like us to become better acquainted before we make love," he said. "Fortunately, I see a solution to the problem." He bent his head and pressed a kiss onto the side of her throat.

Lifting her hands, Sherry rested them against his chest, intending to push him away. But the push never happened. Through his sweater, she could feel the outlines of firmly delineated muscles, and the best she could do was say weakly, "Jean-Claude, don't."

"Don't you want to hear my solution?" One of his hands smoothed her hip—tenderly, as if it were a rare and precious artifact. His other hand crept sneakily up her ribcage until his palm curved around the underside of her breast.

Sherry was having a lot of trouble breathing, and even more trouble thinking straight. "Yes. No. I suppose," she mumbled.

His fingertips grazed the peak of her breast. She inhaled sharply and knew from the throbbing, tingling sensation that her nipple had sprung instantly erect.

It was a tremendous battle, but the sensible part of her won. "Jean-Claude, please stop," she said sharply.

Obediently, he lifted his hand from her breast and stood looking down at her. "My solution is simple . . . Come away with me for the weekend, Chérie. A friend has offered me his beach cottage to use whenever I wish it. We can get to know each other."

The man seemed incapable of going two seconds without touching her. With his fingertip, he drew a line down the curve of her cheek, adding earnestly, "I promise there will be no lovemaking unless you wish it."

A weekend with Jean-Claude? With delicious sensations flooding through her from the touch of his hands, and his dark eyes only inches from hers, all she could think was how wonderful it sounded.

An idyll of laughter and play. A time to talk, to share their innermost feelings. And surely, given their mutual attraction, it would not be long before they made love.

Into her fantasy trickled cold drops of reality. What was she thinking of? Where were those anti-Jean-Claude pills when she needed them most?

Irritated with herself for letting him get to her again, she snapped, "For the weekend? You know that's impossible! There's a recording session for *Guns and Roses* on Monday. I'll be busy all weekend copying your music."

While she talked, she managed to escape him by backing up several steps. It was much easier to be rational when he wasn't touching her, she discovered. But her line of retreat was cut off when the backs of her knees touched the edge of the flowered couch.

He shrugged, again with the Gallic splaying of his hands she found so appealing. "So? Let your partner handle it. Hire an extra assistant or two, if necessary."

Sherry gaped. "I couldn't do that. It wouldn't be fair to Maggie."

His eyes narrowed and he took a step toward her. "Has Maggie never gone off and left you to handle a job alone?"

"Well . . ." Actually, there had been several occasions, the most recent when Maggie had spent a week in Baja with Jake, leaving Sherry to cope with a rush job for a record date.

"As I thought. Have you ever left your partner on her own?"

"Well, no."

"Again as I thought." He took another step toward her, closing the distance between them to a couple of feet. This time there was nowhere for Sherry to go unless she discarded her dignity and scrambled over the back of the couch. "You let Maggie take advantage of you, Chérie."

The man was impossible! Trying to lure her away from her duties, and now criticizing her partner! "That's not true. Maggie's a good friend."

"By her own lights, I suppose she is. However, I take it from something she said that she gave you very little notice before she moved out of the apartment and that she has left you to shoulder the rent alone."

Sherry glared at him. If she could work this into a good argument, surely it would be easier to send him away. "That's none of your business, Jean-Claude."

"No, I suppose not," he said without rancor.

Now he was less than a foot away, within easy touching distance. She might have guessed he wouldn't let the opportunity pass. He picked up her hand and lightly caressed her palm. Bright droplets of pleasure splashed through her.

Damn the man! How did he know so unerringly where to find her most sensitive places? Come to think of it, with Jean-Claude, she was nothing but sensitive places.

"What is my business is to convince you to spend the weekend with me, Chérie." He leaned toward her, his mouth coming close to hers.

She twisted her head away and protested, "I can't."

"Why not?"

"We've gone over that. Because I have a job to do and because I'm a responsible person."

A small frown flickered between his brows. "Perhaps you are too responsible."

Sherry wished she could have her hand back. How could she argue effectively while he persisted in caressing her lifeline? Or was it her love line? "There's no such thing as being too responsible, Jean-Claude."

"There is when you take no time for yourself, when you will not allow yourself any pleasure."

She had to have her hand back; the things he was doing were too distracting. With a wrench, she snatched it away from him and put both hands behind her back. "Pleasure? Is that what's most important to you, Jean-Claude?"

He shrugged. "Most important? I cannot say. But of course it is important. Life is short and meant to be enjoyed."

"We could never get along." *Whoops!* Now she sounded

as if she expected a long-term relationship. She said quickly, "Certainly not for a whole weekend. Our values are simply too different."

"It is a question of values, is it?" His eyes bored keenly into hers. "I insist that we have many values in common. Very important ones they are, too."

"What?" she demanded. "Name one."

He closed the small remaining distance between them. Deliberately, he placed both hands on her breasts and made circles over her nipples with his palms. The yearning shooting through her was so intense she had to lock her knees to keep from collapsing onto the couch.

He lifted his hands from her body and fastened his gaze on her erect nipples, the throbbing nubs clearly visible through her wispy bra and the thin fabric of her bodice. "I see great value in what I can do to your body with my touch."

Intending to use her hands to ward off Jean-Claude's next caress, Sherry took them from behind her back. Instantly, he turned her gesture against her. Seizing her right hand, he pressed her palm against the front of his trousers. In a voice that was husky with desire, he said, "And this. Do you place no value in the force of what you do to me?"

Sherry almost swooned. The frank sexuality of his gesture, the force of his erection burning and pulsing against her hand, the look of unmasked passion in his face, made it the most erotic moment she had ever experienced.

From her head to her toes, flames of desire licked at her. A thick congestion gathered in her lower body, and her breasts ached for Jean-Claude's hands and mouth.

He seemed to be equally affected. His pupils were dilated; his breathing came in ragged, syncopated gulps.

His need poured over her like a can of gasoline thrown onto an already roaring blaze.

If he had been silent, then . . . If he had kissed her . . . But instead he chose to speak in a hoarse, desire-choked voice. "I value such signs as these above all else, Chérie. When it happens between a man and a woman as it has happened between you and me, it is the most priceless thing in the world."

He was twisting her statement about values, corrupting something important to her into just one more seductive ploy, and it affronted her. She managed to cool the blaze in her body enough to say firmly, "Jean-Claude, no more arguments. No more discussion. I want you to go . . . now!"

"Do you mean it?" He let her have her hand back, though her palm felt permanently branded with the shape and hardness of him.

Peering closely at her face, he sighed. "Yes, I see you do." He shoved his hands into his pockets and backed a pace away from her. "Very well, Chérie, but I must warn you, this is only the overture. Our symphony has yet to begin." With great dignity, and looking not at all like a man defeated, he turned and strode to the door.

It took a half hour under a cold shower—a highly overrated cure, Sherry decided—before she cooled down enough to go to sleep.

Chapter 5

"FLOWERS AGAIN TODAY?" Maggie cast an amused glance at the bouquet of violets on Sherry's desk. "Maybe he's losing his touch."

"I hope so," Sherry said fervently. But somehow she doubted it. In the week since her dinner with Jean-Claude, she had avoided seeing him by the simple expedient of sending Maggie to all the recording sessions for *Guns and Roses*.

Unfortunately, out of sight had not meant out of mind. Every day, some reminder of Jean-Claude had arrived at the KopyKats office. First a bouquet of roses with a card saying how much he had enjoyed their evening together—and try though she might, she had been unable to find any irony in the message.

The next day, it was a small teddy bear wearing a beret. The accompanying note said only, "Think of me."

And the next, a tiny music box that played a tune she had heard Edith Piaf sing—something French, of course.

When nothing arrived on Sunday, Sherry hoped the siege was over. But on Monday a bouquet of yellow daffodils was delivered, the card reading, "Thinking of you."

Yesterday had been the worst—or the best, depending on how she looked at it—a sheet of music paper in a simple wooden frame. On the page were a few lines of music and the signature of Benjamin Britten. The note said, "I thought you might enjoy having this."

That one had to go back, much as she would have liked to keep it. A manuscript with the English composer's autograph was too valuable to accept. And while she was at it, she intended to return all of Jean-Claude's other nonfloral tokens.

The reason she had not already done so was lack of time. To make up for sending Maggie to the recording sessions, Sherry had taken charge of the night copying stints. Violet circles beneath her eyes were evidence that the work had taken its toll. But the real problem was that even when she had a chance to sleep, Jean-Claude's laughing eyes and impish grin kept intruding, interrupting her count of sheep.

By day, she suffered from a profound sense of uneasiness, as if a cog in her mental machinery had slipped. Being a clear-headed sort, she soon recognized the cause was a nagging sense of regret.

But it couldn't be that, she kept telling herself, because it didn't make sense. She was convinced she had been right to call a halt to Jean-Claude's lovemaking and that refusing to see him was the wisest course.

Time after time, she had mentally replayed their last conversation, and her conclusion was always the same—Jean-Claude was exactly what she feared, another man like her father and like Mark, with no understanding of duty or commitment.

And even had he been different, there was still the

likelihood he was going back to France at the end of
Guns and Roses. Which wouldn't be long now. Only one
more day until the music was finished.

"By the way," Maggie said brightly, "I was telling
Jake about your songwriting last night. He has some
friends in the music business he thinks might be interested
in seeing your songs."

Sherry looked up. "Thanks, Maggie, but you know
what will happen." She wrinkled her nose as she repeated
the verdict she had heard so many times from producers
and publishers to whom she had sent her songs. "Not
commercial, they always say."

They also usually commented that her songs were
interesting and well constructed. But that, though nice
to hear, didn't matter if they couldn't be sold. Now when
words and melodies bubbled out of her, she knew her
songwriting for what it was—a hobby, a pleasant pastime
but not a potential career.

"I still think you gave up too easily," Maggie insisted.
"But you're probably right about Jake's friends. I doubt
if any of them could help." She paused, then said slowly,
"I'll bet Jean-Claude could do something for you, though.
He must have connections all over. Have you told him
you write songs?"

"Certainly not," Sherry said severely. "And I don't
want you telling him, either."

Maggie sighed. "Okay." She cocked her head to one
side. "You're really determined to avoid the guy, huh?"

"I think it's best."

"And I think you're crazy." With a quick glance at
Sherry's set expression, she added, "Could I make one
little suggestion?"

"Is it about Jean-Claude?"

"Nope."

"Then be my guest," Sherry said magnanimously.

"Don't you think you'd better go home and get some sleep?"

Sherry stretched and said, "I guess I might as well." The parts were already prepared for the following day.

"I think you should. Frankly, partner, you're looking a little worn around the edges."

Just then the sleighbells on the door jingled, and from the doorway came a deep baritone voice. "I do not agree. I think you are looking exceptionally beautiful today." His gaze dwelt on the red sweater Sherry had worn with a red and black watch-plaid skirt. "Red becomes you, Chérie."

Sherry stared. "Jean-Claude!"

As usual, he was casually dressed, in a pale blue V-neck sweater with the sleeves pushed up to the elbows. In the open vee at his chest, a cloud of dark hair enticed her eye to linger. His long and lean lower half was covered by a pair of faded jeans that fit him like a second skin, molding the lines of his trim waist and muscular thighs.

Shutting out the thought of what a pleasant picture Jean-Claude made, Sherry lifted her chin and announced, "I'm very glad you're here, Jean-Claude."

His eyebrows rose; his dark brown eyes sparkled. "So! This is very good news, Chérie. Just when I had begun to think you were avoiding me!"

She ignored his jibe. "Thank you for the flowers and the gifts, Jean-Claude, but I can't accept them. I don't mean to sound ungrateful, but I'm afraid you'll have to take everything back."

He glanced at the dozen red roses, which Maggie had arranged in a vase and placed on the long work table. Miming astonishment, he exclaimed, "You wish to return to me bouquets of wilted flowers, Chérie? Would it not be simpler just to throw them away?"

Sherry gritted her teeth and wondered how he thought he could get away with playing dumb. "I didn't mean the flowers."

"Ah, then you liked the flowers. I am glad to hear it."

From delighted, he flipped abruptly to desolate. "I am saddened you did not care for the other little tokens," he said mournfully.

"It's not that I didn't like them," she began.

He strolled farther into the room. "You did like them?"

"Well, of course I did."

He broke into a broad, lazy grin. "I am delighted to hear it, Chérie. You have saved me much time, you know."

That stopped her. With a puzzled frown etched between her brows, she said, "Saved you time? How? What are you talking about?"

"Why, if you had not liked the things I sent, naturally I should have felt obliged to search for things you would like better."

From behind her desk, Maggie said cheerfully, "Well, if you two will excuse me, I have errands to run and . . . uh . . . errands to run."

"No, no," Jean-Claude said quickly. "Please do not go, Maggie. In truth, I am here because of business."

"Business?" Sherry asked suspiciously. Monkey business, most likely.

"Yes. I fear it is necessary to make a few revisions in tomorrow's music."

She groaned. "You're kidding! We just finished copying it a little while ago."

"Nonetheless," Jean-Claude said firmly, "the producers have recut the scene, so the music must be made a little shorter."

Sherry sighed, then said to Maggie, "I guess you'd better call in the troops."

Maggie reached for the phone, but Jean-Claude forestalled her. "No need. The problem is, I assure you, a minor one. With the three of us working, we should be able to finish in an hour or two."

"The three of us?" Sherry echoed.

"Certainly. I have every intention of staying to help." He included both partners in a broad, beaming smile. "Furthermore, when we have finished, it will give me great pleasure to escort you two lovely ladies to dinner."

An automatic *no* sprang to Sherry's lips, but when she heard Maggie accept, she reconsidered. "Why, yes, thank you Jean-Claude," she said politely. With Maggie along, what harm could there be in a simple dinner?

She might have guessed, with Jean-Claude involved, things wouldn't work out the way she expected. As he'd promised, correcting the music took only a couple of hours. But when they were almost done, the phone rang.

Maggie picked it up, listened for a moment, then said, "Uh-huh. Okay. No problem. Love ya, too."

Jean-Claude had preempted one corner of Sherry's desk, and so was seated only a few feet from her. As they worked, she had been vividly aware of his presence, particularly since his style of copying included a constant stream of little jokes.

It had served to make the time pass pleasantly, but it had also made it hard to concentrate. All she could think of was how nice Jean-Claude was to have around . . . although, catching glimpses of his strong, masculine frame from the corners of her eyes, *nice* seemed far too tame a term.

"That was Jake on the phone," Maggie announced. "He's invited a few friends over to the apartment, so I guess I'll have to renege on dinner. I'm sorry, Jean-Claude."

Sherry lasered a look of reproach at the redhead, but Maggie refused to meet her eye.

"That's all right, Maggie," said Jean-Claude. "Why don't you go ahead and leave? Chérie and I can easily finish the little that is left."

"Gee, that's great. Thanks, guys." Maggie hurried to the door. "Why don't you two stop by later?"

Before Jean-Claude could respond, Sherry looked up from the page she was copying and said, "Thanks for the invitation, Maggie, but I'm planning to make it an early night. A very early night." There! she thought triumphantly. Now Jean-Claude knew she had no intention of letting the evening extend beyond a simple dinner.

Only a few minutes more and they were done. While Sherry ran the duplicates and gathered the acrid-smelling sheets into piles, Jean-Claude leaned against the monster, his arms crossed over his chest . . . watching her.

Each time she bent or turned, she had a definite sensation of eyes—on her hips, her breasts, the curve of her waist. But that was silly. Unless he had developed protruberant, B-movie Martian eyestalks, she couldn't possibly *feel* anything.

"Where to?" she asked when the music was assembled and packed in KopyKats' fiber case.

"I will leave the choice of a restaurant to you, since I am not familiar with the area."

"You mean the *Guide Michelin* hasn't rated any of the places in this neighborhood?"

A grin twitched the corners of his lips. "I fear I left my copy of the *Guide* at home in Paris." He put his finger to his lips. "Never tell my papa or my *grand-père,* Chérie. They would think I had lost my senses. Do you know somewhere pleasant we might go?"

"I think so," she said cautiously. An imp of perversity had gotten hold of her, a tiny demon who had figured out how to frustrate Jean-Claude's plan. No doubt he had in mind a dim restaurant, a few glasses of wine to loosen her inhibitions . . . and then—in for the kill.

With a carefully bland expression, she said, "There's a place quite near here I like. The food is excellent."

"It is not too elegant?" he inquired. "I fear I am not dressed for formal dining."

"Don't worry," she said with a straight face. "You're dressed just fine."

Outside, the winter dusk had given way to dark; around the street lights, halos of mist heralded a heavy fog before morning.

There was time for only the smallest of small talk before they reached their destination half a block away. To give Jean-Claude credit, he only flinched a little when she led him into El Grande, which was primarily a fast-food stand dispensing tacos, burritos, and other Mexican delicacies through a window opening onto the sidewalk; however the proprietors had recently installed small Formica tables and hard-backed chairs in a space equivalent to a narrow hall.

She hadn't exactly lied, Sherry assured herself. The food at El Grande was really very good. It was just that she was pretty sure Jean-Claude had had a rather different sort of place in mind.

If so, he was careful not to show it. With apparent relish, he ate his chimichanga, a deep-fried flour tortilla stuffed with shredded beef. But when he had finished, he wiped his hands on one of the flimsy paper napkins from the dispenser on the table, then leaned back and folded his arms across his chest. "Well," he said, freighting the single syllable with heavy significance.

His voice and the expression in his eyes made Sherry uneasy. Though she still had a couple of inches of burrito left, she put it down on her paper plate and said nervously, "If you're finished, maybe we should go. I've had plenty."

Jean-Claude gave a slow sideways sweep of his head. "On the contrary, I have not finished. I have not even begun."

Without warning, he uncrossed his arms and leaned forward to rest his elbows on the table. Skewering Sherry with his stare, he demanded, "Why have you been avoiding me, Chérie?"

She felt like a butterfly wriggling on a collector's pin. "Wh-what makes you think I've been avoiding you, Jean-Claude?"

He snorted derisively. "Oh, come now. Do you expect me to believe that you have won the flip of the coin every single day for the past week?"

Drat! Why had she ever told him about that accursed coin-flipping? She picked up her burrito, took a bite, and chewed it many more times than necessary. When she finally swallowed, she had made up her mind to tell the truth . . . or at least part of it. She put down the remaining fragment of the burrito and looked Jean-Claude squarely in the eye. "All right, I confess. I *have* been avoiding you."

"Yes, yes, I know," he said impatiently. "But what I do not understand is why."

Wiping her hands on her napkin, she said, "Has it occurred it you, Jean-Claude, that I might be involved with someone?"

"It crossed my mind," he admitted. "But I know for a fact it is not so."

His assurance irritated her enough that she snapped, "Oh yeah? What makes you think you know so much?"

"It is simple." He held up his forefinger. "One. You would not have kissed me with such abandon had you been involved with another man."

"Well, er . . ." Sherry mumbled.

"And two." His second finger snapped up to join the first. "Because Maggie told me you were not involved with anyone."

Sherry spent a few blissful seconds contemplating her redheaded partner squirming in a pot filled with boiling oil.

"So I repeat," Jean-Claude said. "Why are you avoiding me?"

She shoved her plate to the side and matched his posture, leaning forward and resting her forearms on the table. "Has it occurred to you that maybe I simply don't want to get involved with you?"

"Of course, it has occurred to me," he said promptly. "But again, I ask myself why. The chemistry is undeniably there between us."

As if to prove his contention, he reached out and covered her hand with his. The result was inevitable; sensation blossomed through her body like a rose opening its petals in the summer sun.

Heaven help her! Why couldn't she find some way to keep Jean-Claude from touching her? Maybe a suit of armor would do the trick, if she kept the visor lowered and the gauntlets on. She carefully eased her hand out from under his and put it in her lap. It was time for the shock treatment. The notion had formed in her mind that the only way to get rid of Jean-Claude once and for all was to tell him the plain unvarnished truth. She drew a deep breath and said flatly, "All right, Jean-Claude. I'll tell you why I've been avoiding you. The truth is, you're too charming."

He jolted back in his chair, his eyebrows shooting skyward. "There is such a thing as too much charm? I confess, I had not thought of myself as possessing that elusive quality, but I had also supposed it to be a desirable one."

She shook her head. "You don't understand."

"Then you will have to explain it to me."

She swallowed, her mouth suddenly dry. Why was this so difficult? Was it because, once she had finished explaining, she was certain Jean-Claude would give up and leave her alone? Was it possible she didn't want him to leave her alone?

She took a deep breath. "You have to understand, Jean-Claude, I've known men like you before."

"Be careful, Chérie," he warned. "No man likes being put in a category."

"I realize that, and I'm sorry if what I say is insulting. It's just that..." In her efforts to explain, she forgot about keeping her hands under the table. She waved one in a vague gesture and was relieved that for once Jean-Claude made no attempt to capture it. "You see, I'm grown up now. Things like . . . like charm and good looks aren't important to me anymore."

He looked puzzled. "Yes? Do please go on."

"What attracts me to a man now is his character. What matters to me is his dependability and reliability, his seriousness of purpose."

A smile frolicked about his eyes and twitched the corners of his lips. *"Mon Dieu!* This sounds extremely grim."

She gave a triumphant nod. "You see! As I told you last week, our values are just too different." Oh, heavens! Why had she said that? The memory of what that discussion of "values" had led to made a wave of heat rise up her throat and her sweater seemed to lie heavy on her breasts.

Fortunately, Jean-Claude took no notice. "I said your description sounded grim," he replied, "not that I myself am lacking in those qualities you profess to admire. I am, in fact, all those things."

She sat back in her chair and said flatly, "Somehow, I doubt it." That should do it. Surely he would be furious enough to stalk out of El Grande and out of her life.

His reaction surprised her so much a feather could have knocked her off the hard wooden chair. Instead of bristling or stalking, he said thoughtfully, "I see. You question my character. In that case, I suppose I shall have to supply references."

She was again surprised—though relieved, she assured herself—when he walked her back to the office without making a single attempt to touch her. Though he hadn't seemed angry, she must have succeeded in putting him off after all, she thought. At last, he would stop pursuing her.

It was what she had wanted, wasn't it? There was no reason why she should feel so cold and miserable as she climbed into bed.

It was only then, with the covers pulled up to her chin, that she realized that, although she might have succeeded in getting rid of Jean-Claude, she hadn't managed to return a single one of his gifts.

The next morning at the KopyKats office, Sherry shook her head incredulously. "You're not going to believe this,

Maggie." She waved a sheaf of papers she had taken from an imposing legal-looking envelope delivered by special messenger a few moments before.

"What is it? A summons?" Maggie gasped. "Is someone suing us for something?"

"No, it's a packet of testimonials. About Jean-Claude." She couldn't help smiling. "He must have stayed up half the night writing them."

Maggie peered over Sherry's shoulder at the pages. "Do you mean he wrote testimonials for himself?"

"I'd say so," Sherry replied dryly. "I find it difficult to believe he's actually had a long personal acquaintanceship with Minnie Mouse."

Maggie giggled. "Minnie Mouse?"

"Mm-hm. And Smokey the Bear. And James Coburn." How had Jean-Claude guessed she'd had a teenage crush on that particular actor? "And the President. And Casper the Friendly Ghost and a dozen more."

"What do they say?"

Sherry skimmed a representative page, purportedly written by George Washington. "They're all pretty much the same. He's supposed to be dependable, reliable, hardworking. A perfect paragon, in short. Better to have around than a whole troop of Eagle Scouts."

"And you don't believe it?"

Sherry snorted. "Not for a minute! Anyway, I never did trust Minnie Mouse. Her eyes are too beady."

Maggie perched on one corner of Sherry's desk. She had a twitchy air about her that meant she was dying to say something.

"Okay, Maggie, spit it out!" Sherry said at last.

"Well, you're probably going to holler at me for saying this, but you keep smiling at those papers, and you have a funny little gleam in your eye. You may not want to admit it, partner, but I think you're weakening."

Sherry didn't holler. Instead, she fell into deep, silent thought. She'd taken her best shot. She'd told Jean-Claude the bald, unpalatable truth, and it hadn't done a bit of good. Judging from the evidence, he was still in full cry, like an enthusiastic beagle on the trail of a tiring rabbit. Was her nose starting to twitch? Were her ears growing long and furry?

She shivered. "Heaven help me, I'm afraid you're right."

As if it were an omen, a slip of paper sailed from between two of the testimonials. Maggie retrieved it, scanned it quickly, then handed it to Sherry. "Well, it looks as if you're going to have to make up your mind pretty quickly."

The note read: "It would mean a great deal to me if you would come to the session today. Yours—hoping—Jean-Claude."

Maggie said with a helpful air, "If you're going to be on time for the session, you've got about ten minutes to decide how you feel about the guy."

Sherry emitted a heartfelt sigh. "I think," she said to a mystified Maggie, "you may as well just call me bunny."

Chapter 6

AT THE STUDIO, Sherry handed the music over to the librarian, then went into the main room to watch for Jean-Claude.

Admitting to herself she was weakening had unleashed something in her. Bubbles of excitement were rising in her blood; she felt as giddy as a teenager going out on a first date with the most popular boy in school.

She was also as nervous as a teenager. Half a dozen times, she smoothed her hand over her slim navy-blue slacks or tugged at the lapels of her matching blazer.

And then, at last, Jean-Claude came through the double doors carrying a leather briefcase. For this final recording session, he had dressed a little more formally than was his wont, in pleated, ivory slacks and an ivory jacket over a midnight-blue shirt.

When he saw her, he stopped dead and a smile blossomed across his features. Plunging forward, he hurried across the room so fast she thought he might be planning to sweep her into his arms.

But a scant foot away, he stopped and set down his

briefcase, then bathed her in a gaze so warm it sent waves of delicious weakness flowing outward from her midsection.

Sherry was grinning like a fool. Finally, she managed to say faintly, "Good morning, Jean-Claude."

"Chérie." He breathed his version of her name, then seized her hand in both of his. "You came," he said simply.

"Yes, I did." Her voice had developed a betraying tremor.

"How delightful!" His grip on her hand tightened. "I am glad you are no longer avoiding me."

She would have made an airy gesture, except that Jean-Claude had her hand and was caressing the back of it with his fingertips. "Oh, well," she said, "after all those glowing testimonials, I figured I must owe you an apology."

One of his eyebrows tilted upward. "So you have changed your mind about my character, have you?"

She hadn't. Not really. But her objections just didn't seem to matter very much anymore.

"With all those famous people speaking out on your behalf, how could I quibble?" she said brightly. "There's just one thing. I don't understand how you got to be such friends with Minnie Mouse."

He let go of her hand and said straightfaced, "Madame Minnie is a frequent guest at my family's restaurant."

"But you didn't mention Mickey. Wasn't he with her?"

"No, not of late." He put a finger to his lips and whispered, "Not a word, Chérie, but I fear there may be trouble brewing between those two."

Sherry looked shocked. "Good heavens! I had no idea."

"You will not tell?" he asked anxiously. "I would not want to be responsible for a leak to the press."

"I won't say a word," she said solemnly.

The long hand of the clock on the wall ticked toward the vertical and the noise-level in the room rose bit by bit as the musicians warmed up on their instruments or practiced difficult passages from the music to be recorded that day.

A jeaned and T-shirted studio technician wheeled a video monitor into place near the central podium, a sign that some of today's music was not rhythmic enough to be synchronized to beats clicked into the musician's headphones. Those parts of the score would require Jean-Claude's skilled hand and eye to coordinate the music with the images on the screen.

He observed these marks of activity and said, "In a moment, I must go, Chérie. There are a few things I must discuss with the engineer before we begin."

"Of course. Go right ahead, Jean-Claude."

"In a moment. First..." He paused, his eyes fixed on her face as if weighing her probable reaction. "Perhaps I am pushing my luck, Chérie, but do you recall that little beach cottage I mentioned to you before? Will you ... would you perhaps reconsider going there with me this weekend?" He finished in an earnest rush, "It is important to me that we spend time together and get to know each other."

She blinked, taken aback. "You're rushing me a little, Jean-Claude," she said uneasily. "Can't we take it one step at a time?"

A faint frown flickered between his brows. "One step at a time. Yes, I suppose we can do that, although..."

Although what? Sherry wondered. His impatience was flattering, no doubt about it, but why couldn't he give her a little time?

His frown vanished. "Then I suppose the first step is

to be certain you will stay for the entire session. And since we have only half a day of recording to do, the next step is to ask if you will join me for lunch."

"Yes, I'd like that, Jean-Claude," she said with pleasure.

"Ah, bien! And after that, perhaps we might spend the afternoon together. And after that, dinner."

"Wait!" She laughed and held up her hand like a traffic cop. "That sounds like three or four steps to me."

He pulled a face of mock chagrin. "Ah, you noticed!"

"I certainly did."

"Well, then, I will just have to try again—later."

He accompanied this statement with such an alarming waggle of his brows that she chuckled and shook her head. "Jean-Claude, you're impossible."

"Impossible to resist, I hope."

She pursed her lips and made herself look prim. "Nothing is impossible, Jean-Claude."

Purposely misunderstanding her, he leered. "Nothing? You give me great hope, Chérie." He glanced up at the wall clock. "Now I really must go. We will continue this discussion of what is possible and what is not after the session is over."

"That is it. Thank you very much, ladies and gentlemen," Jean-Claude said to the orchestra. "You are all marvelous musicians and I am extremely pleased with what we have done here."

The orchestra broke into enthusiastic applause, and Sherry joined them, clapping her hands together so hard her palms stung.

Hearing Jean-Claude's music had awed and delighted her even more than at the first session of *Guns and Roses*. He was a major talent, she had concluded, and with any luck should soon join the ranks of those film composers who commanded the highest fees and whose scores were automatically considered for Academy Awards.

The morning had provided a feast not only for her ears, but also for her eyes. Watching Jean-Claude conduct the orchestra, with his easy stance and clean, economical use of the baton, she had felt herself weakening more and more with every minute. Not only was he handsomer and more charismatic than any man had a right to be, he had made it plain he wanted her with a single-minded determination that sent thrills of excitement rushing through her blood.

Now he held up one hand in an effort to get the orchestra's attention. When at last it was quiet, he announced, "You are all invited to stay and listen to playbacks of the music. And . . . there is champagne in the booth."

That was enough to scatter the orchestra. Jean-Claude stepped down from the podium and hurried to Sherry's side. Draping his arm lightly around her shoulders, he said, "A brief delay in our plans, Chérie. I promise we will not have to stay for long."

"I don't mind, she said with a smile. "I think it's going to be fun."

It *was* fun, she decided a short time later. Jean-Claude had gotten her a glass of champagne in a plastic cup, but was soon torn away by two bankerish-looking types from the JRA production office. To her amusement, Sherry found the two men in their three-piece gray suits virtually indistinguishable, and mentally dubbed them Tweedledum and Tweedledee.

The booth was jammed. Bodies were smashed up against the leather-padded recording board, with its hundreds of dials, buttons, and sliding levers, and were packed sardinelike all the way to the back wall, where the studio's gold and platinum albums were displayed.

Presently, music poured out of the overhead speakers and the conversation level dropped to a manageable hum. Sherry sipped her champagne and made small talk with several of the musicians, but her eyes kept returning to Jean-Claude.

He stood near the center of the booth talking to Tweedledum and Tweedledee. As she watched, he threw back his head and laughed, his fine tanned throat rising above his collar. Even though she hadn't heard the joke, Sherry felt like joining in the laughter. In fact, she felt unusually giggly, she realized.

She eyed her champagne glass with suspicion and found it nearly empty. It was funny, she thought. Drinking champagne at midday was something she had never tried before; the effect was really quite interesting.

Clutching her empty glass, she listened to the music for a while longer. Then she felt a touch on her waist and turned her head to find Jean-Claude standing very close. The warmly intimate look in his brown eyes sent harplike glissandos running up and down her spine.

She unfolded a beatific smile. "Jean-Claude, I haven't told you how wonderful your music is." Or how delightful it was to have his arm curved protectively around her waist.

He gave a quick shake of his head. "Be careful, Chérie! You will give me an enormously swelled head." From behind his back, he produced a green-tinted bottle. "Mademoiselle, a little more of this excellent champagne?"

"Not too much." She held her glass out and giggled. "Jean-Claude, I'm surprised at you! You must know this champagne is terrible!"

"Yes, it is," he agreed as he half filled her glass. "But

oddly quite enjoyable, under the circumstances."

Sherry took a sip. "Mm. It's a funny thing, but you're right. It seems to get better all the time."

"Have some more." He hoisted the bottle and, before she could protest, filled her glass to the rim.

She waggled a reproving forefinger at him. "Jean-Claude, are you trying to get me drunk?"

He dropped his arm from her waist and grinned. "Heaven forbid! I am only trying to make you feel relaxed."

"Oh, I'm relaxed, all right." Maybe too relaxed, she thought. The nearness of Jean-Claude, his warmth, and the musky aroma of his after-shave were loosening the little restraints that kept people from doing silly things. For instance, she had a notion it might be nice to throw her arms around Jean-Claude's neck and kiss him, right in front of all these people.

Get a grip on yourself, Sherry.

He slipped his arm back around her waist and pulled her close. His breath was a delicious tickle against her ear. "Is it possible you are now relaxed enough to accept my invitation for the weekend?"

"So that's why you're plying me with champagne! That's pretty sneaky, Jean-Claude."

"It's not sneaky if I admit it," he pointed out.

Each time he brought up the subject of the weekend, his plans sounded more and more appealing. She let out a faint sigh and wondered why she even bothered trying to postpone the inevitable. The way things were going, it was almost a foregone conclusion that sooner or later— probably sooner—she would end up in his bed.

And then what? She wasn't too tipsy for some measure of rational thought. She sipped her champagne and looked at him over the rim of her glass. "The truth is, I'm not sure I want to indulge in a..." She hesitated, then finished bluntly, "A weekend fling."

The smile died from his eyes; his brows lowered to a straight forbidding line. "A weekend fling? Who said anything about a weekend fling? Surely, I did not."

"No, you didn't, but..." She broke off, then blurted, "You haven't actually said much of anything else about your plans, either."

He replied gently, "Forgive me, Chérie, but it seems a bit premature to speak of a long-term commitment."

Sherry recoiled and felt the fringes of a blush trailing across her cheeks. "Oh, good heavens, Jean-Claude! All I meant is that I don't even know if you're planning to stay in L.A. now that the film is over."

He went very still. For one awful moment, she thought she knew what he would say—that he was going back to France. But he had also said it wasn't a weekend fling he had in mind. It didn't add up.

His smile seemed a little forced, but Sherry forgot about it as soon as she heard his words. "Ah, as to that, let me assure you that my intention is most definitely to make my career here in Los Angeles. Does that answer your question?"

The rush of relief she felt was staggering. "Yes. Yes it does. It's possible..." she said, trying to sound judicious when she felt anything but, "if you were to ask me again to go away for the weekend, I might say yes."

His entire face lit up with delight. His eyes danced and his lips curved, the narrow grooved dimple at the corner of his mouth leaping into prominence. He slid his arm back around her waist, his fingers fanning out on her ribcage. "Ah, Chérie, I am beginning to think that with you and me, anything and everything is possible." She stared back at him raptly. "We will go away tonight," he went on. "Or this afternoon. Right away, as soon as we can decently leave the studio. I promise you it will be wonderful. We will—"

How he would have finished, she never learned, for a voice hissed, "Jean-Claude, I have to talk to you." Sherry snapped her head around to find Andrew Watson glowering at them.

Jean-Claude dropped his arm from her waist. "What is it, Andrew?"

With a glance at Sherry, Watson reiterated in peremptory tones, "I have to talk to you . . . alone."

"There is nothing you cannot say to me in front of Miss Seaton," Jean-Claude said with a frown.

Watson's chest expanded, then deflated. Arrowing an anxious glance toward the far end of the booth where Tweedledum and Tweedledee stood, he whispered, "The island battle scene, Jean-Claude. What tape is it on? The guys from the production office want to hear it, but the engineer can't find it in his log."

Swift thoughts played across Jean-Claude's face, then resolved into a grim headshake. "There is no island battle scene."

Stark terror peered out of Watson's eyes. "There has to be. It was added in the recut that was done just the other day."

"If this is true, then I was never informed."

"Of course you were informed. You must have been."

Jean-Claude's face worked furiously, and he seemed about to make an angry retort. Then, with iron control, he said flatly, "I was not informed. If you wish to dispute this, we will check the list of changes I was given and you will see that I am right. However, this is a small matter at the moment. The question is, what is to be done?"

"Done?" Watson seemed on the verge of gibbering. "What can be done? We have no options. We have to have the scene."

"If we must have it, we must," Jean-Claude said with strained patience. "I will have to write it, Miss Seaton's firm will have to copy it, and the orchestra will have to be called for another day to record it."

Watson looked as if he were coming apart. "But, Jean-Claude, you don't understand. In order to make deadline, the music—all the music—has to be finished by to-morrow night."

It was amazing how fast she could go from tipsy to stone-cold sober, Sherry observed an hour later. Of course, she had had plenty of incentive. If ever there had been a music-business equivalent of the cry "all hands on deck and man battle stations," that was what had happened at the studio.

Much as she disliked the man, she had to give Andrew Watson credit for moving into action. Somehow, he had gotten Tweedledum and Tweedledee out of the booth without their learning of the disaster, then had galvanized the contractor, the man in charge of hiring musicians, with a brief word. There and then, he had rehired all the players still in the booth, and seconds later was on the phone to the answering services that handled most Los Angeles area musicians, rounding up the rest of the orchestra.

Sherry didn't know what had happened after that, because she herself had left for the KopyKats office in order to alert Maggie to the emergency, send out the call for assistants, and check their supplies.

Fifteen minutes after she got there, a video monitor

and VCR arrived, dispatched from Andrew Watson's office—for it had been decided that Jean-Claude would work at KopyKats, where each page he completed could be handed immediately to the copyists. The video equipment was needed so he could view and review the now-notorious island battle scene.

Five minutes after that, Jean-Claude himself walked in. The ebullient, laughing man of the party had vanished. This Jean-Claude had a bleak face and a tiny muscle pulsing in his jaw.

As soon as the office door closed behind him, he spewed out a torrent of rapid French, his tone leaving no doubt of his sentiments. Two assistant copyists looked up in alarm, and Sherry hurried across the room to meet him.

He grimaced apologetically. "I am sorry, Chérie. It's just that I cannot believe this has happened. It is Watson's fault, of course. The man is an imbecile. I cannot understand why he has kept his job."

She gave him an anxious look. "How bad is it, Jean-Claude? Is it a long scene?"

"Seven minutes" was his terse reply.

She gasped, "Seven minutes!"

He nodded. "Unfortunately, the scene has almost no dialogue, so the music must carry the emotional weight of the story."

Horrified, she stared up at him. The way Jean-Claude described it, the scene would be thick, lush, and dramatic, the most difficult and time-consuming kind of music to write. "But that's impossible," she blurted.

For the first time since entering the office, Jean-Claude smiled. Leaning forward, he brushed a kiss onto the tip of her nose. "We decided earlier, did we not, that nothing is impossible. Don't worry, Chérie, it will be all right."

Slowly, she said, "Jean-Claude, couldn't you just refuse to write this scene?"

"Of course I could refuse. My contract protects me from such things. But if I do not compose the music, some *hack*—"he very nearly spat the word—"or two or three, perhaps—would be hired to do it." He hesitated, then added on an apologetic note, "I realize this ruins our plans, Chérie, and ensures that today and tomorrow will be very long and very exhausting. Would you have liked it better if I had refused?"

"No, I wouldn't," she said honestly.

"Good. I am glad to hear it, because this is something I must do. It is . . ." He drew a deep breath. "It is a matter of integrity, do you see?"

She looked at him, pride and satisfaction swelling in her breast. He didn't know it, but he had just destroyed her last reservations. The lightweight, undependable charmer she had thought him would have refused the grueling labor he now faced. *That* man would have been content to let someone else finish the film. *That* man would have shrugged and taken the easy way. And *this* Jean-Claude was not, after all, that man!

With a great rush of pleasure and relief, Sherry decided she could let nature take its course. If she fell in love with him, it would be all right.

Chapter 7

"THIS IS A cottage?" Sherry stared incredulously through the car window at the two-story house with its red-tiled roof and walls of white stucco. Beyond was the blue-green shimmer of the sea and the white sand of a deserted beach. "It looks like a mansion to me."

Jean-Claude cast a quizzical look at the ornately carved front door. "In truth, I had not expected anything quite so grand."

It was late afternoon on Friday, and the music for *Guns and Roses* was finally finished. During the long day and night in the KopyKats office, Jean-Claude had worked with the stamina of half a dozen lesser men, his pencil flying as if self-propelled over the yellow score paper.

It was nearly dawn when he ripped the last page from his pad and stood, stretching to relieve cramped muscles. He crossed the room to Sherry's desk and asked quietly, "Can you take a short break?"

She had slept for a few hours during the night, while

Jean-Claude had not, but was still well ahead on her share of the copying. She nodded and, when he suggested going outdoors, slipped into her coat and went with him.

There was something about coming out into the dawn after a night of work that had always struck Sherry as special and rare, as though the world had been freshly created, especially for her. Standing beside Jean-Claude on the deserted sidewalk, she savored the birth of the day and took in a great gulp of air not yet tainted by the city's fumes.

Making it only fractionally a question, he said, "We will leave this afternoon as soon as the session is over."

She had answered simply, "Yes." The minute the island scene was recorded, they had left for Santa Barbara.

Jean-Claude hoisted their bags from the trunk of his car, a small rented Mercedes. At the front door, he inserted a key into the lock. But before he could turn it, the door was pulled ajar from the inside. Viewing them with frank curiosity was a round, middle-aged lady with graying blond braids circling her head. "Yes? What is it?"

His eyes widened in surprise. "Is this the home of M'sieu Parsons?"

"Yes."

"In that case, I believe we are expected. I am Jean-Claude Delacroix, and this is . . . ."

The woman broke into a broad smile. "Oh, yes, Mr. Delacroix. Mr. Parsons told me you were coming for the weekend. Landsake, I didn't expect you quite so early, though, with the traffic so bad on Fridays and all. Of course, you could have got here any time. With Mr. Parsons away so much, about all I have to do is keep things ready for his guests." She paused for a gulped breath, then said, "Landsake, I didn't introduce myself, did I? I'm Mrs. Hanson, Mr. Parsons's housekeeper."

She seemed to have run down. With faint worry lines cluttering her brow, she studied Jean-Claude and Sherry, then said slowly, "Mr. Parsons didn't mention you'd be bringing Mrs. Delacroix."

Sherry opened her mouth to explain, then thought better of it and was relieved when Jean-Claude supplied smoothly, "A last-minute change of plans." He added with a smile, "Mr. Parsons also did not mention that so lovely a lady would be in residence at his beach house."

The housekeeper dimpled, obviously disarmed. But Sherry thought, if Jean-Claude's friend *had* mentioned Mrs. Hanson, they probably would have chosen to go elsewhere. A weekend with a middle-aged, possibly pur-itannical housekeeper lurking about was not what she had in mind.

Of course, Jean-Claude hadn't said what *he* had in mind. But from the way he had looked at her during the drive, reaching over to touch her hand or her knee, or smooth back a blowing tendril of her hair, she thought she had a pretty good idea.

The housekeeper led them upstairs to a room that was a miracle of air and light. Apart from a few touches of blue-green bringing the sea and the sky indoors, it was furnished all in white. White eyelet curtains rustled gently in the salt breeze from the ocean. In the center of the room stood a wide, white, billowy bed.

The bed seemed to draw Sherry toward it . . . like a cloud she could sink into and sleep and sleep and sleep. Its wide, white comfort made her newly aware of her scratchy, reddened eyes and the leaden fatigue of her muscles.

She took one longing step toward the bed, then stopped as Jean-Claude lifted their suitcases onto folding stands Mrs. Hanson had produced from the closet. Should she give in to her tiredness or battle against it? What would Jean-Claude want? Would he expect to make love at once?

He snapped open the locks on his leather bag, then turned to Sherry, a frown crinkling his brow. "I hope you don't mind my letting Mrs. Hanson think you are my wife, Chérie. It seemed easier that way. But if you would rather have a separate bedroom, I will explain."

"Just how would you explain that, Jean-Claude?" she teased.

"I will tell her that I snore," he said promptly.

Deliberately, she widened her eyes. "Good heavens! *Do* you?"

"Not to my knowledge."

She considered for a moment and decided it would be hypocritical to opt for separate rooms. "It's all right," she assured him.

"It is more than all right." He crossed the room and dropped his hands onto her shoulders. In a low, husky voice, he said, "Ah, Chérie, I can scarcely believe that at last we are alone together."

He bent his head and kissed her briefly, the warm motion of his lips making her wonder if she was really as tired as she thought. But when the kiss ended, a vast yawn overtook her. Though she tried to cover it with her hand, Jean-Claude saw it and smiled. "You are tired, Chérie?"

"A little," she admitted.

"So am I." But he didn't look tired. His eyes were as bright, his shoulders as straight as if he had had a full night's rest. "I am sorry, Chérie. I fear I am exhausted."

She suspected him of making a gentlemanly gesture and bestowed on him a grateful smile. Although she was certain making love with Jean-Claude would be wonderful no matter what the circumstances, within her was a deep well of fatigue she feared might damp the joy of their first encounter.

"Get ready for bed, Chérie," he instructed her. "I will go downstairs and ask Mrs. Hanson to make sure we are not disturbed."

It seemed as if he was gone for a very long time. Sherry took a shower and slipped into a soft cotton nightgown. Sinking into the billowy bed, she made determined efforts to stay awake until Jean-Claude returned.

"Chérie?"

She forced one eye open and saw he had a bounce in his step and a smile in his eyes. "Um?" she said dreamily.

"It seems we will have the house to ourselves after all, at least at night. Madame Hanson has her own apartment over the garage."

As she let her eyelids sink, her lips curved in a dreamy smile. Alone. She was alone with Jean-Claude. "That's nice," she murmured through the fog in her brain. Seconds later, she slipped into a deep, dreamless sleep.

She awoke to moonlight streaming through the windows and the sound of the surf beating a subtle rhythm in her ears. Beside her was the warm presence of Jean-Claude.

Turning on her side, she found him watching her, his face tender and yet composed, as if he had been watching her for a long, long time. When her gaze met his, his face tautened in the moonlight, and awareness flared in his eyes like the leaping of a candleflame. He made no move to touch her, but said evenly, "You are awake, Chérie."

"Yes." Her voice emerged as a husky throb. "So are you, I see."

That he was awake was not all she saw. The sheet was pushed down to his waist, baring his broad, muscled shoulders. His bronzy tan was silvered by moonlight, and a cloud of dark, silky-looking chest hair tapered slightly to the point where the sheet covered him.

Studying him, she felt a slow pulse of excitement start beating in her blood, a growing awareness of his body, so close, so strong, so vibrantly masculine.

In tones that were casual yet held a tight thread of meaning, he asked, "Are you still very tired, Chérie?"

Deliberately, she reached out and put her palm flat on his chest, savoring the tickle of his hair against her skin. With the touch, his muscles bunched, and he took a sharp gulp of air into his lungs.

"It's a funny thing, Jean-Claude," she said with a lightness that failed to conceal her own growing difficulty in breathing. "I'm not at all tired anymore. Not the slightest bit."

Clearly accepting her words as the invitation she had intended, he groaned and reached for her. He seized her body with fierce possession, molding her curves against him. Into her hair, he muttered, "Ah, Chérie, it seems I have waited forever for this moment."

The sheet had bunched between them while they slept. Without releasing her, Jean-Claude pulled it out of the way. She felt the full, hard length of him pressed against her and discovered he was naked; her flimsy cotton gown was the sole remaining barrier between them. The shape of his desire pressed against her belly sent a shudder of longing through her, a fluttering hunger that loosened her last constraints and made her pliant in his arms.

He pulled her higher on the bed, positioning her so their mouths were only a breath apart. His lips softly edged hers open but he lingered at the threshhold, teasing her lower lip, then her upper, in a long, unbroken series of kisses that left her breathless and eager for more intimate contact.

Finally, he probed deeper. The plunge of his tongue unlocked a bold sensuality in her, and she returned thrust for erotic thrust, her senses blooming like tropical flowers, lush and ripe with the promise of passion.

Moaning softly, he reached for the hem of her nightgown. As she twisted sinuously to ease his task, the touch of the cotton sliding up her body echoed the seductive caresses of his hands. The sheets whispered of ecstasy as he threw them back to bare her body to his ardent gaze.

"Ah, Chérie." His gaze fastened on the full rise of her breasts, their tips already puckered with desire. Delicately, he touched one peak, then the other. The hand that had been cramped around a pencil for so many hours had lost none of its facility, for he skillfully drew her nipples into aching pleasure points crowning the apexes of her swollen breasts. As he continued to caress her, explosions of desire followed a powder trail down her body to unite in a wind-fanned blaze centered at her feminine core.

Suddenly, surprising her with the urgency of her need, she could think of nothing but igniting Jean-Claude with the same urgency that tormented her. Boldly, she lifted her shoulders from the pillow, reached low on his body, and cupped her palm over the thrusting shape of his maleness.

His groaned "Chérie, Chérie" made her smile with

pleasure. Wantonly, she ran her hands over his naked body, delighting in the smooth resilience of his skin, testing the tautness of sinewy muscles from his hair-roughened chest, down over a flat, hard belly to the sturdy power of his thighs. At last, her hands returned to the center of his masculinity and its throbbing leap between her palms loosed in her sharp arrows of desire.

"Stop!" he commanded, and seized her wrists in his hands. In a gentler voice, he said, "It is too much, too soon, Chérie. If you continue, I fear I will lose control."

She wanted him to lose control, she silently protested. She was ready for him to claim her completely, to begin the wild ride into ecstasy.

But in the next moment, she began to learn how much she owed to Jean-Claude's restraint. Sitting cross-legged beside her, he positioned her on her back and proceeded to compose a symphony on her skin.

His fingers performed taunting, tumultuous melodies on her breasts, a song soon echoed in a deeper, more demanding key by the hungry tugging of his lips. One hand danced lower, writing cascades of notes on her belly and thighs until she arched her hips, her legs sliding apart to welcome him.

He found the place between her thighs where she thrummed with want and elicited powerful chords of satisfaction with the deftness of his touch. But even with this pleasure singing through her, her desire was reaching a pitch of need requiring resolution.

She wanted him. She needed him now, she thought helplessly. But all of her was bound up in her senses; she was silenced by the writhing flames that consumed her, her mind engulfed by the erotic movements of his mouth and hands.

At last, Jean-Claude broke the spell. An agonized groan broke from deep in his chest. "Chérie . . . I must . . . I cannot . . ."

With that, she found her own voice. "Jean-Claude, please. I want you."

In a hasty scramble, he moved himself over her, his face raw with hunger. Even then, he managed to contain himself. For a moment longer, he poised above her, delicately testing her readiness to accept him. Then, with a great sigh of mingled agony and ecstasy, he thrust into her, filling her with throbs of rapture unlike anything she had ever imagined.

As he established a rhythm that matched her own unspoken wants, wild words of adoration tumbled from his lips. Although the muttered endearments were in French, their meaning was clear; no barrier stood between them any longer.

Skin to skin, body to body, soul to soul, they climbed together, rhythms and needs matching as though this were not the first but the hundredth time they had been together.

In unison, they reached a place where words could not go, where rhythm broke into disjointedness, a tumbled place, noisy with inflamed passion. Rocking together, their motions now dictated by a crazed drummer, they flew out of time and into an ecstasy of release. She was a scant step ahead, but then, with a last stroke, a final drumbeat, he joined her, shuddering and gasping out her name.

For Sherry, there was a long spiraling down into quiet while she savored Jean-Claude's weight on her softened breasts. Finally, he eased away from her. Lying on his side, he gathered her against him and held her as if she were infinitely precious to him, all the time murmuring endearments into her hair.

She was dreamily boneless and drifting, twining against Jean-Claude, her satisfaction so complete she could not imagine anything but this state of total satiation. Sometime later, she said as much to him.

He pulled back from her, laughing, one eyebrow raised. "Are you challenging me, Chérie?"

She shook her head and protested, "No, no. Really, I'm not. It was just so incredible, I can't believe I'll ever . . ." She let her voice trail away, leaving the rest to his imagination.

His smile faded. He ran one hand over her hip in a tenderly soothing motion. "Chérie," he said in a low, soft voice, "what you are feeling, I feel also. This exhaustion of the senses is, I believe, the ultimate experience between a man and a woman. It is the sign of a profound joining, more than most people ever experience in their lives."

She looked at him, her eyes filled with wonder, her heart filling with love. "Is that what it is, Jean-Claude?"

"Yes. Trust me. I know, though I, too, am a stranger to this peace." Gently, he rested his hand on the undercurve of her breast. "But I also know something else, Chérie. The pleasure and the passion are very close, waiting for us to tap them again at any moment. Even now, perhaps."

Her smile was dubious. She was certain that, despite Jean-Claude's potent effect on her, it would take a long long time for her sleeping desire to reawaken.

As if he read her mind, he shifted his hand so his palm centered on her nipple. A sharp tingle surprised her; a hint of warmth flickered in her center.

She lifted her head and looked down at herself. Seeing

the pucker of her uncovered nipple, feeling the tug of new desire in her loins, she said sharply, "I don't believe it. It's impossible."

Jean-Claude bent his head and grazed her breast with his lips. Against her swelling peak, he murmured, "Don't you remember, Chérie? With us, nothing is impossible."

Chapter 8

IN A PALE pink kimono, Sherry stood by the bedroom windows and watched the shimmer of sunlight on the waves. The beach was deserted, the sky the pale blue of a clear winter morning.

She had awakened, a few minutes before, glad to find Jean-Claude still asleep. She needed a little time alone to try to get the night before into perspective.

It was no surprise to discover she had fallen deeply in love with Jean-Claude. For days, she had been veering in that direction. All along she had guessed that once they made love, she would lose her heart.

What *was* surprising was the vein of wanton sensuality he had tapped, turning sedate Sherry Seaton into a bold and demanding femme fatale. After making love a second time, they had slept. But then, sometime in the night, real caresses had stolen into her dreams and she awoke, throbbing with desire. That time, she had done things she had never even dreamed of . . . and had gloried in the doing.

Sherry stole a quick glance at Jean-Claude. He was no longer sleeping but lay on his back with his elbows bent, his fingers laced beneath his head. His eyes were wide open and he was watching her with a little smile tugging at the corners of his lips.

"Uh-oh!" she murmured. Damn! What *did* one say the morning after when one had behaved like Sheena the Jungle Girl the night before?

He let out a lazy chuckle. "Uh-oh? What kind of thing is that to say to your lover, Chérie?"

"Um, what I meant to say was good morning." Double damn! At least she could have come up with something brilliantly witty.

He seemed not to mind the feebleness of her dialogue. "And a very good morning to you, Chérie. Did you sleep well?"

"Very well." And next they'd be discussing the weather or something equally inane. "Amy Vanderbilt ought to write a book about situations like this," she muttered.

Jean-Claude looked first startled, then alarmed. "The woman who gives advice in your newspapers? Is something terribly wrong, Chérie?"

Sherry smiled. "You're thinking of Dear Abby. Amy Vanderbilt writes about etiquette. And I wish she'd covered this, um, situation. I guess I'm feeling a little nervous."

"That is because you are too far away, Chérie. I, too, feel a little nervous—or perhaps discontented—when I cannot put my arms around you or hold your hand." He patted the side of the bed. "Come sit beside me, and we will both feel better."

Gingerly, she took a seat beside him, then realized she might have known Jean-Claude wouldn't leave it at that. Leaning forward, he slipped his arms around her and pulled her against his chest. "Now explain to me why you are nervous, Chérie."

The warmth and reassurance of his touch dulled the keenest edge of her embarrassment. "Actually, I was mostly embarrassed, Jean-Claude."

"So?" He looked astonished. "What could you have to feel embarrassed about?"

She mumbled against his chest, "I'm afraid I went a little crazy last night."

His chuckle was soft and reassuring. "Then you must have taken another lover while I slept. I remember no craziness at all, only the most wonderful, passionate, giving woman it has ever been my privilege to know. You are much woman, Chérie."

She looked right at him, the last traces of her shyness shredding and blowing away on the wind of his approval. "And you are much man, Jean-Claude."

He dropped a kiss onto the tip of her nose, then said thoughtfully, "Do you know, I think I like it that you felt a little awkward with me this morning? It means you are not blasé about our lovemaking." He smoothed one hand gently over her back, then under her arm to brush the side of her breast. "Ah, Chérie," he murmured.

Sherry felt two conflicting sensations—one, the first stirring of desire, and the other the realization that her stomach was screaming for food.

Jean-Claude's hands moved to the knot in the sash of her kimono. She clapped her hand over his industrious fingers. "I think you'd better stop that. I'm starving. Do you realize we never had dinner last night? I'm not even sure we had lunch. Or breakfast, for that matter."

He put one hand over his heart and said mournfully, "You break my heart, Chérie. Surely, if I were a truly great lover, I would be able to distract you from such a minor matter as food."

"Me you could distract," she admitted. "But my stomach refuses to pay attention." As if in agreement, it grumbled. "See?" she said lightly. "Dibs on the first shower."

By the time she had toweled herself dry and dressed in faded jeans and a yellow tank top, she had generated an idea that pleased her greatly. She was going to cook breakfast for Jean-Claude.

It wasn't very emancipated of her, she realized as she tripped downstairs—giving in to a primitive urge to provide sustenance for the man she loved. But who cared? And besides, now was the perfect time, since breakfast was the one meal she could handle without fear of disgracing herself.

At least she thought she could.

Now, if she could only find the kitchen...

Following a hunch, she turned down a hall leading to the back of the house. She pushed open a swinging door and found she had guessed correctly. With gleaming terracotta tiles, stainless steel appliances, and hanging copper pans, it was a kitchen right out of *House Beautiful*—except for the plump, aproned figure of Mrs. Hanson standing at the sink.

Sherry froze in the doorway. Good Lord! She had completely forgotten the housekeeper's existence. Now what?

"Good morning." Mrs. Hanson wiped her hands on a towel and straightened her apron. "So you're up, are you? It's a beautiful day, isn't it? And what would you and your husband be wanting for breakfast, Mrs. Delacroix? There's just about anything you could name. Mr. Parsons likes me to keep a well-stocked larder."

Sherry stepped all the way into the kitchen and let the

door swing shut behind her. "I was wondering, Mrs. Hanson. Would you mind awfully if I did the cooking this morning?"

Worry lines formed on the housekeeper's brow. "Well, I don't rightly know what Mr. Parsons would say if I let a guest do my work." She studied Sherry's face and her forehead smoothed. "Bless you, child. You two are newlyweds, aren't you? And you want to cook for your man."

Sherry nodded, ignoring the pang of guilt she felt for continuing to deceive the housekeeper. "I'd really like to."

"I know exactly how you feel, child. I felt the same way myself when Hanson and I were first married." Untying her apron, she finished briskly, "Leave the cleaning up for me, though. That way, I'll feel like I did part of my job."

Sherry grinned. "Mrs. Hanson, that's the best deal anybody's offered me in ages."

Deciding on the menu was easy for one of Sherry's limited abilities. Omelets were always good and fairly reliable. Orange juice, of course. Bacon and toast. She could handle all of those, she was certain.

Her surprise for Jean-Claude got off to a good start. He pushed open the kitchen door and sniffed ostentatiously, then planted his hands on his hips. "You are a horrible liar and a fraud," he said severely. "You told me you couldn't cook."

She waved a mitted hand at him. "I told you I *didn't* cook. There's a difference. Besides," she finished candidly, "breakfast is about the extent of my repertoire."

"Can I do anything to help?" he asked.

"Not a thing." The table was set with flowered place

mats, bacon sizzled in a skillet, the toast was in the toaster and the omelet was all mixed and ready to pour into the pan.

"But, Sherry . . ." He wore a little frown; she couldn't think why unless it was because he wanted to horn in on her act.

"Just sit down, Jean-Claude," she said firmly. "Breakfast will be ready in a minute."

A brunette waitress filled Jean-Claude's coffee cup, then hoisted the pot in Sherry's direction.

"No, thanks," she said glumly. She rested her elbows on the Formica tabletop and propped her chin in her hands. "I still don't understand how everything could have gone wrong."

"Not everything, Chérie. The omelet was delicious."

"Oh, sure!" she scoffed. "If you like your eggs rare." The omelet was the only thing that had turned out underdone. The bacon was nearly black before she'd noticed it, and while she was lamenting this mishap, great clouds of smoke started pouring out of the toaster.

Jean-Claude had been kind and supportive, insisting that he liked his bacon ultra-crisp and that all the toast needed was a little scraping. However, she couldn't help noticing how relieved he looked when she elected to give up the whole project and take him out for breakfast—after first hiding the awful evidence from Mrs. Hanson.

She grimaced ruefully. "The thing is, I really can cook breakfast. At least, I thought I could."

She was still despondent as they drove out of the parking lot. But a few moments later, she brightened and pointed out the car window. The street was lined with houses, now converted to shops, in the California bungalow style of the years before World War I. "Oh, look, Jean-Claude! It's the antique district. Can we stop and browse?"

He glanced at his watch and seemed to calculate something. "Of course. If you like," he said, and steered the car into a vacant space at the curb.

Predictably, browsing with Jean-Claude turned out to be fun, with him threatening to make a present to her of a life-sized dressmaker's dummy or a red-and-white-striped barber pole. Though she never actually saw him buy anything in the shops they visited, when they were back in the car he reached into his pocket and pulled out a small circular object, done up in paper. "This is for you, Chérie."

She opened the package to find a delicate, old-fashioned cameo. "It's beautiful, Jean-Claude. Oh!" She frowned. "You shouldn't have. You've already given me far too many presents."

"Mere trinkets, nothing more," he said, waving away her protest.

Her frown deepened. "They weren't trinkets. That Britten manuscript must be valuable. I don't think it's right for me to keep it."

His shrug was nonchalant. "Of course you must keep it. I have another manuscript signed by the maestro. I would like you to have that one, Chérie."

"At least I should have bought *you* a present."

He silenced her with a long, heart-stopping kiss, then murmured, "Chérie, don't you know that your presence with me this weekend was the greatest gift anyone could have given me?"

His words touched her heart as his kiss had stirred her body, and she longed to be alone with him, to show him in every way she could think of how deeply she cared for him. "Shouldn't we be getting back?" she suggested shyly.

He agreed enthusiastically, but as soon as they reached the beach house, he excused himself, saying he had a couple of calls to make and would use the telephone in the study. It was half an hour before he emerged, looking strained and unhappy. He waved away her questions with a smile and the explanation that it was only a small business problem worrying him.

During lunch—served by Mrs. Hanson on the terrace jutting out onto the sand—he became his old merry self. When they finished eating, he announced that after the strenuous morning they had spent, they needed a nap.

Of course, napping wasn't at all what he had in mind. This time, their lovemaking began as a delightfully silly affair, with lots of giggling and clamping of hands over each other's mouths for fear Mrs. Hanson might hear.

Inevitably, the laughter ended and the afternoon evolved into slow, languid hours of mutual discovery, interspersed with times of quiet conversation.

Late in the day, Sherry stretched like a satisfied cat, then rolled over onto her stomach and wrapped her arms around the pillow. "I feel so . . . wonderful," she said dreamily.

Jean-Claude's fingertips touched the tops of her shoulders. "This will make you feel even more wonderful," he said, and kneaded deep into her muscles, loosening them to a state of fluid comfort.

Sherry sank deep into a happy golden haze, pierced at last by Jean-Claude's voice. "Are you awake, Chérie?"

"Just barely."

"Then perhaps this is not the time to ask . . ."

She snuggled deeper into the pillow. "Ask away," she murmured vaguely.

"I cannot help wondering why you have never told me about your marriage."

"Um . . ." She had to struggle to force herself alert. "I don't know. We just haven't been together enough to get around to talking about it, I guess."

That was odd, she thought. She and Jean-Claude hadn't spent much time together, and yet she felt as if she had known—and trusted him—forever.

"Is it painful for you to talk about?" he asked.

"No, not anymore. What would you like to know."

His hands went on manipulating her shoulderblades. "You are not the kind to give less than your best to anything you try, so I am certain the divorce could not have been your fault. He was unfaithful to you?"

"No." She thought for a moment. "Actually, he was unfaithful, but since I didn't find out about it until after the divorce, that wasn't the problem."

He continued his ministrations. "Then what was the problem?"

"Different standards. Different needs." She told him a little about Mark's career and how it had gotten in the way of their marriage.

When she had finished, he said, "But why was this a problem?"

Sherry was sinking deeper into drowsiness. Talking about Mark wasn't keeping her awake, because she no longer cared, even a little, she realized.

It seemed too complicated to explain the role played by Mark's basic lack of commitment, so she chose the simplest explanation that was still the truth. "Because I needed to be settled. I need an orderly life, Jean-Claude. When Mark was working, he was gone for long stretches of time. I couldn't handle the loneliness." She paused, then added, "Long-distance relationships never do work out, do they?"

His tone was noncommittal. "I suppose."

"Anyway, the only way it could have worked was if I'd been willing to go with him, but I couldn't do that." A yawn interrupted her. When she continued, her voice was slurred. "I guess I need a certain amount of stability in my life. A lot of stability, actually. Maybe that makes me an old stick-in-the-mud and a stay-at-home, but that's the way I am."

Jean-Claude's hands stopped moving on her back, than lifted away from her. She was too drowsy to fully register his withdrawal until he said, "Chérie! There is something I should tell you."

"Um?" She rolled over and curled up on her side with her eyes closed. "What is it, Jean-Claude?"

He was silent for a long moment. When he spoke, his voice sounded as if it came from a long distance away. "Never mind. You are falling asleep and it is not important."

She felt the bed dip and lift as he swung his legs over the side and stood. "Are you going somewhere?" she mumbled into the pillow.

"More telephone calls," he said. "It is nothing to worry about. Go to sleep, Chérie."

Mrs. Hanson cooked them a delicious dinner and blushed like a girl when Jean-Claude praised her culinary skills. After the housekeeper retired to her own apartment, Sherry and Jean-Claude prowled around the big house, not snooping into anything private, just marveling at the fine furnishings bestowed on what was, after all, only a vacation home.

The living room was the one room furnished too starkly for Sherry's taste; it was done all in sand tones except for the gleaming black grand piano against one wall. Jean-Claude's eyes lit up when he saw the instrument. "There! That is the only thing I have been missing. Shall we make a little music?"

"You go ahead. I'll be the audience."

She curled up on one end of the sand-colored couch and listened with pleasure to Jean-Claude play a Chopin nocturne and one movement of a Mozart piano sonata. Then he stood and lifted the lid of the piano bench. "Look, Chérie. Here is some music for piano, four hands. You must join me."

Her piano-playing was adequate, but it would be a struggle keeping up with Jean-Claude. She said as much, then added, "It's too bad I didn't bring my guitar. If I had it with me, I'd be happy to do my stuff."

Jean-Claude exclaimed, "But there is a guitar here! I saw it upstairs in one of the guest rooms."

"You're right. It was in the small room at the front of the house, wasn't it?" She jumped up from the couch. "Do you think your friend would mind if I played it?"

"I am sure he would not."

She ran upstairs to fetch the guitar and came back to the living room, running her hands over the polished wood. "It's a beautiful instrument," she said as she tuned the strings to a note from the piano.

She took her turn as performer with several haunting Appalachian folk songs. When she had finished, she waved away Jean-Claude's compliments and insisted, "Now we have to do something together."

In the piano bench, they found a book of old-fashioned favorites, and that was how they ended the evening, with "Harvest Moon," and "Old Folks at Home," and finally,

"Good Night, Ladies." Sherry's fragile, sweet soprano soared over Jean-Claude's husky baritone.

"I don't know when I've had such a lovely day," she said as she put her hand in Jean-Claude's to climb the stairs.

"You will see, Chérie. Tomorrow will be just as wonderful." He stopped mid-staircase to press a quick, warm kiss to her lips. "Because we'll be together."

It turned out he was absolutely right. They arose late, having lain awake for a long time the night before, talking and making love. After a late brunch, they went out onto the beach. Barefooted and with their trousers rolled to midcalf, they strolled down the sand to a spot where some college kids were playing volleyball. Invited to join the game, they played for a while.

The nicest thing about that interlude was Jean-Claude's apparent blindness to the golden-skinned beauty who had the college boys falling all over themselves.

"The, uh, blonde was very attractive," Sherry observed as she and Jean-Claude left the game.

Jean-Claude scowled. "That overgrown football player fellow in the red trunks? You thought him handsome?"

She let out a little chuckle. "*Him?* I meant *her*. The girl in the blue bikini."

At that, Jean-Claude threw his back head to laugh. "So you were jealous, Chérie. How marvelous!"

"You were jealous, too," she pointed out.

Arms around each other's waists, they wended an unhurried course back the way they had come. But as they neared the house, Sherry sensed a slight withdrawal from Jean-Claude. His eyes were remote; a smile no longer sprang so readily to his lips.

"Is something wrong?" she asked as they climbed the steps to the terrace.

He glanced at his watch. "I'm afraid I must make more phone calls. It is that same business I mentioned yesterday. Can you amuse yourself for a while?"

"Of course," she said promptly, relieved it was only business bothering him and nothing to do with her. "I think I'll take the guitar out on the beach and play for a while. It's too nice a day to stay indoors."

"I shouldn't be long. I will join you on the beach when I am through." Pulling a small leather notebook from the hip pocket of his jeans, he headed toward the study.

Sherry took the guitar and wandered out onto the sand. Sitting cross-legged, she strummed the chords of a few old favorite folk songs, singing softly to herself. But then, new chords began to evolve under her fingers; hints of a new melody slipped into her brain. She let herself go with it, experimenting with one phrase, then another, and was delighted to find scraps of lyric that seemed to fit.

After half an hour, she knew she had done all she could with the song for the moment. She was pleased with what she had. It was different, stronger and more sure, than anything she had written before. What it was— she realized, unsurprised—was a love song for Jean-Claude.

She no longer had the slightest doubt that she loved him. Several times, the night before, she had longed to blurt out her feelings, but had held back, wanting him to be the first to mention love.

Smiling to herself, she idly strummed the strings. She couldn't be certain how he felt, not until he spoke, but she was convinced he cared for her. They were so in tune with each other, mentally and physically, that moving on to something more permanent could only be a matter of time.

Time. The thought triggered an association, and she began singing a song she had written several years before, so engrossed in the words and music that she was not aware of Jean-Claude until he stood beside her.

She broke off mid-phrase and looked up at him with a smile. "How did your phone calls go? Did you get your business taken care of?"

Ignoring her questions, he demanded, "What was that you were singing, Chérie? I did not recognize it."

"You couldn't. The songwriter is a complete unknown." He lifted his brows and she explained simply, "Me."

"You did not tell me you were a songwriter."

"It's only a hobby."

"That song did not sound like one written by a hobbyist. Will you sing it for me, from the very beginning?"

"Well, I . . ." She shrugged. "Sure, if you want me to." She put her hand on the strings, ready to begin.

"One moment." Jean-Claude glanced quickly toward the house. "Let me get a towel to sit on, so we do not get covered with sand."

"I'm already sandy," she pointed out.

"But I am not."

It seemed unlike him to be so worried about a little sand, but he was soon back, carrying not only a red-and-white-striped beach towel, but also a beach basket with an extra towel bulging out of the top. He set the basket down between them and said gravely, "Now, please, I would like to hear your songs."

He kept her at it for a long time, calling for another song as soon as each was done. Finally, she protested,

"I've done all my best ones. Besides, my throat is getting dry."

Jean-Claude gave a nod of agreement. Standing, he put a hand down to pull her to her feet. "Very well. In any case, it is time to change for dinner. I have told Mrs. Hanson I am taking you out this evening."

Upstairs in their bedroom, he embraced her. "Thank you for letting me hear your songs, Chérie. They are lovely. You have a genuine gift."

She smiled and started to say something like, "Aw, shucks," but he silenced her with a long, spine-tingling, pulse-galloping kiss.

Breaking away, he looked solemnly down at her. "Over dinner, there are things we must talk about, Chérie."

Little frissons of excitement agitated her nerve endings. What could he want to talk about except their future? "What sort of things?" she asked, trying to look and sound calm.

"At dinner," he said firmly.

In a state of high anticipation, she showered and dressed in her nicest dress. A fine, soft jersey in pale blue, it had rows of tiny tucks descending from a yoke at the neckline and a wide, sashlike belt.

With her cheeks flushed from the outdoors, a touch of mascara and lipstick was all she needed . . . those and a hairbrush to discipline her freshly washed hair as it dried. But the hairbrush was nowhere to be seen.

She called into the bathroom where Jean-Claude was shaving, "I can't find my brush. Is it in there?"

"No, it is not," he called back. "Perhaps Mrs. Hanson tidied up while we were out."

"I bet you're right. That woman does too good a job," she grumbled.

The brush was neither in the dresser nor in her overnight bag. That left only Jean-Claude's suitcase. She opened the lid and there it was, sitting on top of a bright-colored, envelope-sized folder of a familiar type.

Not fully conscious of what she was doing but shadowed by dread, she picked up the folder and opened it. Inside, as she had expected, she found an airplane ticket.

It was made out in Jean-Claude's name, for a flight from L.A. International to Charles de Gaulle Airport in France. The time on the ticket identified the flight as departing very late at night. And the date was . . . today.

A wave of cold trembling took her, and icy shock flooded her mind. Jean-Claude was leaving. He was leaving tonight. And he'd had neither the kindness nor the decency to tell her the truth.

Chapter 9

JEAN-CLAUDE CAME out of the bathroom with a maroon bathtowel wrapped around his waist. Diamond droplets of water glittered in the dark hair on his broad chest. His legs were strong and muscular, with beautifully sculpted knees and ankles.

With the ticket folder still clutched in her nerveless fingers, Sherry looked at the body of the man who had shown her ecstasy and was unmoved. How could he not have told her? How could he have let her think he was staying?

His eyes lit on the folder and he froze. Sherry stared coldly at him, wondering how she was supposed to react. Three choices came to mind: She could weep and wail; she could scream at him; or she could brain him with the nearest large object . . . something roughly the size of the dresser.

The last seemed most appropriate until a fourth option flickered into focus. Yes, that was it. If it killed her, she would make Jean-Claude think she was unfazed by his leaving.

It was too late to pretend she hadn't seen the ticket. Carefully, she placed the folder in the exact center of the dresser top and said, "I'm sorry, Jean-Claude. I didn't intend to snoop."

It wasn't a great start, but it would have to do. She brandished her hairbrush at him. "See? I found it in your suitcase. Mrs. Hanson must have put it there." She peered at the tortoise shell brush as if she had never seen it before. "Come to think of it, I can see why she might have thought it was yours. I mean, it's not pink or flowered or anything."

There! That was much better! If she could only keep up the flow of trivialities, Jean-Claude would never suspect how wounded and betrayed she felt.

Lifting one arm in an imploring gesture, he took a step toward her. His towel came undone and fell in a maroon heap at his feet.

This was too much! The sight of him magnificently naked nearly destroyed her. She inhaled a short, sharp gulp of air and said with false brightness, "Whoops! Looks like you lost your towel."

He shrugged, his nakedness somehow not detracting from his innate dignity. "What difference does it make?"

These were the first words he had spoken since she found his airplane ticket and they seemed symbolic of the chasm yawning between them. What difference did it make that he had made her fall in love with him and now was leaving? To him, obviously none.

In order to avoid looking at the rest of him, she focused on his face and saw something there that didn't square with indifference. His eyes were shadowed, and taut creases pulled at the corners of his mouth. He said dully, "I was going to tell you at dinner."

Wasn't that big of him! she thought bitterly. He had

little choice; in order to make his plane, they would have to leave Santa Barbara soon after they had eaten.

She couldn't keep looking at him without letting her pain and anger show. Her hair, falling in damp strings around her face and shoulders, provided the perfect excuse to turn to the mirror over the dresser—and away from Jean-Claude. Lifting a wooden arm, she tugged the brush through her hair and said lightly, "Tell me? Oh, you mean tell me you were leaving? It does seem to me you might have mentioned it." Hastily, she added, "Of course, it's really none of my business, is it?"

He moved around behind her so his face, filled with entreaty, was visible in the mirror. "But it *is* your business, very much your business, especially after this weekend. I intended to tell you yesterday, and again today. But the time never seemed right." He reached out and touched her shoulder with his fingertips. "Please, Chérie. Look at me, let me touch you while I explain why."

"No!" Her voice too sharp, she jerked away from his hand. She swallowed and waved the brush at him. "I mean, go ahead and explain if you want to, but I have to brush my hair out or it'll dry in tangles."

He was silent for a moment; then he moved around to the side of the dresser. "I am leaving only because I long ago made a commitment to score a film in Paris. Tomorrow is the latest I can arrive and still complete the work before the recording date."

The brush tore painfully through a tangled clump of hair. She winced, but managed to say evenly, "I see." But she didn't see why he hadn't told her. What she *did* see was that her first impression of Jean-Claude had been the right one. Getting involved with him had been a disastrous mistake, falling in love with him an even worse one, and she was likely to go on paying for it for a long, long time.

She went on brushing and forced a cheery veneer over her voice. "It's nice you have a film to do so soon after *Guns and Roses*. You're really going to make a name for yourself, aren't you?"

His face was intent, almost suspicious, as if he didn't believe what he was hearing. He said insistently, "Chérie, please listen to me."

"I am listening." Her hair was tangle-free now, but she went on brushing it anyway.

"You may be listening, but I do not think you are hearing me. The many phone calls I have made were because I was trying to postpone the film." Raw misery peeped out of his eyes. "Unfortunately, it was impossible. I even thought of breaking my commitment, but that is something I cannot do, no matter how much I would prefer to be with you." His voice rising, he finished, "I do want to stay. You must believe that."

She'd heard similar words before, from her father and from Mark. "I wish I could stay longer, sweetheart," and "Sorry I have to go, babe." They didn't mean a thing.

"Well, those are the breaks I guess, Jean-Claude. I just wish you'd told me, that's all." She started lightly enough, but an edge of honest bitterness crept into her tone. She bared her teeth in what she hoped passed for a smile. "I mean, because I . . . I was planning to invite you to a party next week."

"A party?" He sounded incredulous.

"Of course, it's no big deal."

"No big deal," he murmured reflectively, then went on in a rush, "It was a grave fault in me that I did not tell you I would have to go away for a while. But I feared that if you knew I was leaving, you would not have come away with me, and we would not have had this time together."

She felt her lower lip start to tremble and clamped her mouth firmly shut until she got it under control. "Oh, I don't know," she said, trying to sound judicious. "I probably would have said yes, anyway. After all, what's a little weekend fling between friends?"

Jean-Claude's face worked furiously. "A weekend fling! *Dieu!* You bring that up again!" Something in him seemed to snap. His arms went around her and he pulled her hard against him. "You do not mean this, Chérie. You are not a weekend fling to me, and I am certain— no matter what you say now—that I mean more than that to you. Please believe me, I am coming back as soon as I can."

Standing motionless in the circle of his arms, neither striking out nor sagging against his chest, was one of the most difficult things Sherry had ever done. "Well, that's nice," she said in a brittle voice. They always said they would come back, she thought. And sometimes they actually did return. But in the meantime...

She had to get away from him. She was too aware of his clean, male scent, of his warm nakedness so close to her. She put her hands on his chest and pushed lightly. He resisted for only a moment, then dropped his arms to his sides.

Her smile was so wooden she felt as if her face might crack. "Why don't you call me when you get back to L.A., Jean-Claude?" she trilled. "Maybe we can get to-gether."

His face contorted, then he gripped her shoulders and demanded, "Why are you pretending to be so hard and unfeeling? If you are trying to torture me, you are suc-ceeding."

"Why would I want to torture you, Jean-Claude?" Why not, after what he had done to her? But despite her anger, it was hard to ignore the warmth of his hands penetrating her thin jersey dress. She stiffened, fearing she might dissolve into tears.

His hands tightened convulsively, his fingertips biting into her flesh. "You are pretending not to care," he grated. "But I know you care. You could not have been as you were in my arms if you had no feeling for me."

She looked up at his face; it was so strained and unhappy that, against all reason, she felt sorry for him. "You want me to admit I care? All right, Jean-Claude, I'll admit it. I do care about you." With her words, cracks widened in her carefully constructed defenses; she could feel the muscles of her face start to give way. Hastily, she added, "It would be fun if you were going to stick around for a while longer."

"Fun..." He looked down at her, suspicion rampant in his eyes. "Fun," he repeated. "Yes. Very well. At last I see what you are doing, Chérie."

"Doing?" She opened her eyes wide. "I don't understand."

"Yes, you do. You understand perfectly and so do I. But I do not like it much. I think it would be better if you would yell or hit me."

She managed to shrug. "Why on earth would I want to do that?"

Slowly, he said, "Because I am certain you are very angry at me, Chérie, as you have every right to be. It was a risk I chose to take because I did not want to tell you until I was absolutely certain I had to go. I did not want to spoil this magic time for us."

But it was spoiled, she thought unhappily. The magic was gone, no matter what he said and did now. She made her expression carefully blank. "You know what, Jean-Claude? This conversation is starting to go in circles."

He dropped his hands from her shoulders and stepped back a pace. "I have one more thing to say and I will say it, whether you wish to hear me or not. I am coming back. As soon as possible. And not for you, but for myself. And one thing more..." He stopped abruptly and dropped his gaze, shielding his eyes with his lashes. The corded muscles of his neck and shoulders leaped into prominence and quivered beneath his skin.

It seemed a very long time that he stood there, silent and taut with strain. Finally, he gave a tiny shake of his head. His next words startled her, because, spoken in a solicitous voice, they seemed to come out of nowhere. "What would you like to do now, Chérie? Would you like me to take you home at once? Or shall we have dinner before we drive back to Los Angeles?"

His silence had given her the time she needed to reassemble the pieces of her cracked façade, so it was relatively easy for her to say, "Oh, dinner by all means, Jean-Claude. Why ever shouldn't we?"

They ate at a reputedly fine seafood restaurant, though Sherry was in no position to judge, for she mostly pushed the crab casserole around on her plate and never tasted the few bites that reached her mouth. She was too busy glittering. She shone and sparkled. She laughed over nothing. She made brightly amusing remarks, despite the fact that for once Jean-Claude did not hold up his end of the repartee.

Finally, she managed to draw him out about his upcoming film. Although his responses were perfunctory, at least the conversation served to fill the time until they left the restaurant.

They said good-bye to Mrs. Hanson and thanked her

for her kindnesses. That part was all right, but the drive down the coast was not. Sherry's glitter was wearing off, and awkward silences kept creeping into the conversation. The fact of Jean-Claude's departure lay like an ugly, misshapen thing in the space between them. Finally, she escaped by pretending to sleep.

He "woke" her not far from her apartment. With an unfamiliar diffidence, he said, "How would you feel about driving me to my plane? If you would rather not, it is all right. I can leave my rented car at the airport."

Even though she loathed the idea of having to actually watch him go, the habit of pretended indifference was on her so strongly that she said, "If you want me to, I will."

L.A. International Airport was too bright and too loud. Jean-Claude handed his bag over to a skycap and they went to check the ceiling-high computer that listed gates and departure times.

Sherry found herself walking through the crowds with exaggerated care, as if something inside her had broken and had to be protected from further harm. What she needed, she realized, was to be alone somewhere so she could cry, mourn her loss, and storm out her anger at Jean-Claude.

To her vast relief, his flight was leaving on time. She glanced past him at the security gate. "You'd better go, Jean-Claude. You don't want to miss your plane."

A painful spasm rippled his features, then passed away. He said gravely, "I had hoped we would have more time to talk, but I suppose this is neither the place nor the time to say everything that must be said between us."

The neon lights in the terminal dazzled her eyes and mercifully blurred his handsome features. She bit her lip and said nothing.

He went on with restrained urgency, "With luck, I will be gone for no more than two weeks. I will telephone you, *ma petite*, and write letters." He paused, then asked hesitantly, "Will you write me, Chérie?"

She should tell him no, she thought. She should refuse to read his letters or accept his calls. But despite her angry disappointment, she could not quite bear to cut the final tie. She nodded and said reluctantly, "Yes, I'll write."

He bent to brush a kiss onto her cheek. Feeling his warm breath on her skin, imbibing his heady masculine aroma, she wanted to cling to him and cry, "Don't go." But she was past the point of clinging or crying. Her role demanded that she bid him a studiedly casual farewell, then turn and go.

That was what she did. She was composed as she told him good-bye and left the terminal. But when she reached her car, she leaned her head against the steering wheel and cried and cried.

Maggie stepped in the back door of the KopyKats office and frowned. "What on earth are you doing?"

Sherry had her feet up on her desk and her guitar in her lap. She had brought the instrument to the office, thinking that when she had nothing else to do she would fill the time by songwriting. Anything was better than staring into space, brooding about Jean-Claude.

"I'm working on a song," she replied.

"All about heartbreak, I suppose," Maggie scoffed. She sat down at her desk and swiveled her chair to face Sherry squarely. "I haven't said anything until now, but I've been worried about you, partner. It's not like you to mope."

Sherry swung her feet to the floor and protested, "I am not moping." She was very proud of herself. Jean-

Claude had now been gone for a little over three weeks—not two, as he had promised—and she hadn't brooded for a minute. At least, not in public.

Maggie said carefully, "Okay, so you're not moping. Maybe. But something's sure bothering you. And I don't get it. As far as I can tell, you've heard from Jean-Claude just about every day since he's been gone."

Up to a point, Maggie was right. For the two weeks Jean-Claude had said he'd be away, Sherry had received postcards, letters, or phone calls from him nearly every day; but they had been no substitute for his presence, and their content had often added to her frustration. It was as if she and Jean-Claude had become polite strangers, forced to communicate for reasons neither of them understood: He told her the film was going well and that Paris was cold and wet; she told him KopyKats was busy and L.A. was clear and dry.

Nonetheless, hearing his voice, seeing his written words, had been lifelines to Jean-Claude that now had snapped. A full week had passed with no explanation of why he had not returned on schedule. And without a word.

His silence had left Sherry floundering in uncertainty. If he did come back—which she was beginning to doubt—should she let their relationship pick up where it had left off? If she did, what was to prevent him from leaving again? And again after that, plunging her into another endless cycle of brief joy followed by lonely misery, like the ones she had learned from her father and from Mark.

With determined cheerfulness, she told Maggie, "You're a little out of date. I apparently fell out of favor sometime last week."

"Really? I hadn't realized." Maggie frowned, then

brightened as the phone gave a preliminary jingle. "Hey, maybe that's him now."

"It's much more likely to be a customer," Sherry pointed out. She picked it up and said, "KopyKats." In the background was the hiss of white noise she had learned signaled an overseas call. Her fingers tightened on the receiver, and despite her negative musings about Jean-Claude, her heart turned over and flopped like a gaffed fish.

A female voice said, "I have a person to person call for Miss Sherry Seaton."

"This is she," she said breathlessly.

"One moment, please, while I connect your party."

Sherry clasped the phone, her pulse thudding in her ears and a lump of anticipation filling her throat. But the voice, deep and gifted with a French accent though it was, was not the one she had hoped to hear. "Miss Seaton, this is Henri Bonchamps. I am a friend of Jean-Claude Delacroix."

She slumped, the air rushing out of her lungs in a whoosh of disappointment. But in the next second, she straightened, pricked by fear. "Has something happened to Jean-Claude?"

"As far as I know, he is fine, though I have not spoken with him for a week or two." Sherry relaxed, and the voice went on, "I should explain I am a song publisher. I would like to talk to you about handling some of your songs."

Confused, she narrowed her eyes at the phone. "I don't understand, Mr. . . . Bonchamps, was it? You're interested in my songs without ever having heard them?"

"But I have heard them," he said promptly. "Jean-Claude gave me a cassette he made, with you singing your own compositions. I must tell you, Mademoiselle Seaton, that although your songs are not strictly commercial in the American sense, I believe there may be a place for them in the European market."

"Really?" Her mind was working double-time, sorting out what must have happened. Was it possible Jean-Claude had recorded her songs without telling her, that day at the beach? Yes, of course. There must have been a cassette recorder in the beach basket he had placed next to her.

The Frenchman went on, "There are at least three songs on this tape I would like to handle, and I would like very much to see anything else you may write."

Sherry lifted her chin, excitement dimming the gnawing ache in the middle of her chest, where thoughts of Jean-Claude seemed to torment her most. "That's very interesting, Mr. Bonchamps. Can you explain how this would work?"

She emerged from the conversation with a verbal agreement and the promise of a written contract to follow in a few days. Excitement bubbled out of her as she told Maggie the news. But later that day, she was struck by the timing of Henri Bonchamps's call. Into her brain came the nasty, sneering thought that Jean-Claude might have done this for her because he felt guilty. Was it a payoff for favors received as, in an earlier age, a man might have sent jewelry to a discarded mistress?

So sickening was this notion that Sherry began to tip over from uncertainty toward deciding what she had to do if she ever heard from Jean-Claude again.

Hear from him she did, via telephone, three days later in the KopyKats office. His voice sounded tense and hurried. "It is Jean-Claude. I am in New York."

Was she supposed to jump for joy, she wondered, because after ten days of silence, he had finally decided to get in touch?

"Chérie, are you there?" he said loudly. "Can you hear me?"

"Yes, I can hear you, Jean-Claude."

"Ah, *bon!* I am in the airport in New York. I must go or I will miss my plane to L.A."

To L.A.? So he was coming back. And he probably expected that to solve everything, she thought bitterly.

She murmured something noncommital and he hurried on, "*Hélas,* as soon as I arrive, I have a meeting at JRA. But I will see you tonight. Tonight at your apartment. Eight o'clock."

She wasn't sure how to respond, but it didn't matter, because, before she had a chance to speak, there was a click on the line, followed by a dial tone. Jean-Claude had hung up.

"While you've been gone, I've given this a lot of thought, Jean-Claude. Naturally, I appreciate what you did to help with my songwriting, and I'll always treasure the time we spent together, but I don't think there's any point in picking up where we left off."

It was almost eight and Sherry addressed her reflection in the bathroom mirror. In order to be sure Jean-Claude couldn't sidetrack her, she had memorized her speech, complete with oratorical gestures, to the point that it was beginning to sound overrehearsed.

Her decision was no spur-of-the-moment one. From the very first, the logical and sensible part of her had known it was folly to get involved with Jean-Claude. Not hearing from him for all those empty days and nights had merely made her logical voices louder and more insistent.

The bottom line was that she couldn't live with another off-again, on-again relationship, one in which all the commitment was on her side.

Ending their relationship was the right thing to do, she assured herself when the doorbell rang.

Positively the right thing, she thought as she crossed the living room and unhooked the chain from the door.

But then he was standing there, tall and handsome despite his rumpled tan jacket and the dark stubble shadowing his cheeks and chin.

She wasn't aware that he moved. One second he was standing in the hall and the next he was inside, his arms tight around her.

She seemed to be laughing or maybe crying. Her head was pressed against his chest and she could feel that his trembling matched her own shaking weakness. His cheek was pressed against her hair and his breathing was erratic.

He just stood there, holding her and holding her until, finally, her mind lurched into gear. This wasn't how it was supposed to go. She had a speech to deliver.

Pulling back against the restraint of his arms, she knuckled the sting of tears from her eyes and said in a sharp, determined voice, "Jean-Claude, please let go of me. There's something I have to say."

He pulled her back to him and cupped one hand around the back of her head. "Before you say anything, a single word, there is something I must say to you." He paused, then rasped in a emotion-thickened voice, *"Je t'aime,* Chérie."

But that meant . . . It couldn't mean what she thought it meant. A new onset of trembling shook her and a great lump rose in her throat. "Wh-what did you say?"

The pressure of his arms tightened, molding her against him as if he intended their two bodies to merge into one. *"Je t'aime*. I love you, Chérie."

Chapter 10

ALTHOUGH HE HAD said it three times, in two different languages, Sherry still couldn't believe she hadn't misunderstood. "What did you . . . Do you mean . . .?" she stammered.

"I mean that I love you." He looked down at her, a tiny smile lifting the corners of his lips. "You seem surprised, Chérie."

As an understatement, that qualified for the *Guinness Book*. "I am, I guess," she said weakly.

"You should not be. In truth, Chérie, I believe I fell in love with you that very first day, merely from hearing your voice on the telephone. Before I returned to France, I was within a soupçon"—to illustrate, he held up his thumb and forefinger with almost no space between them—"of being certain enough to speak. But things were going so badly between us, I decided to wait." He paused, then said earnestly, "While I was gone, missing you so, I grew certain." He shifted his hands to her waist and finished with determined lightness, "There you have it, Chérie, my heart to do with as you will."

All she could think of was how she had ached for him during the last endless days and nights. She gave a baffled little shake of her head. "When I didn't hear from you for so long, I thought..."

He lowered his brows, hooding his eyes. "Ah, yes. I am sorry, Chérie. There was no time to call or even to send a brief note. I might have sent a telegram, but in truth I did not think of it."

A dubious note crept into her voice. "You were that busy with the film? Did something go wrong?"

"No, it was something else that prevented me from staying in touch with you." He swayed a little on his feet; only then did she realize his usual sparkling vitality was absent. Beneath the surface bronze tone of his skin was the gray pallor of fatigue. "May I sit down, Chérie?"

"Yes, of course." She gazed at him, concerned. "You're exhausted, aren't you?"

"It is nothing. Merely a touch of jet lag." Taking her hand, he drew her down onto the flowered sofa. "Chérie," he began gently. "The reason I did not write or call was because during the last days of the film, my grandfather had a heart attack."

She gasped, lanced by guilt. All that time she'd felt sorry for herself and angry at Jean-Claude, he had been facing tragedy. "I'm so sorry. Is he... Will he be all right?"

He said soothingly, "*Grandpère* is doing well. The doctors say that with proper care, he will live many more years. But for days the family was in an uproar. There was no time to write or call." He slipped his arm around her shoulders. "Now, Chérie, I believe you had something to tell me."

The content of her speech flashed through her mind. Uneasily, she realized that little had really changed. He hadn't said he would never leave her again; he hadn't said anything about the future.

But he *had* said he loved her. He had made a considerable commitment; surely that made all the difference?

She looked at him and loved him—and decided not to tell him how close she had come to ending their relationship. "I wanted to..." she began slowly, then picked up momentum as she thought of what she *could* tell him. "...to thank you for giving my songs to Henri Bonchamps. Do you know, he actually thinks they might sell in Europe?"

"I am glad, Chérie. Henri is a good man. He will do his best for your songs." He looked closely at her, plumbing the depths of her eyes with his chocolate-brown gaze. In a low, soft voice, he said, "Do you realize I have not yet kissed you?"

There were things she wanted to ask him, things she needed to know about his plans. But he was back and had said he loved her, and her apprehensions would just have to wait. "It had crossed my mind," she said, and tilted up her face to welcome him.

At first, it was a gentle kiss of greeting, his lips moving smoothly on hers and his hand threading through her hair. After a long time, he said quietly, "I am so glad to be back, Chérie. I missed you so."

"I missed you, too," she whispered. "I..."

She was going to tell him she loved him, but he bent his head and covered her mouth with his. His tongue twined with hers in a sinuous duel that left her breathing raggedly. His hands skimmed her hips, her waist, her breasts, until pulse points of desire throbbed a rhythmic tattoo in her body.

With a groan, he wrenched his mouth from hers, then slipped one arm around her shoulders, the other beneath her knees. Lifting her, he stood. Seemingly without effort, he carried her to her bedroom, where he deposited her gently on the edge of the bed.

In the faint yellow glow of the bedside lamp, he took a cursory look at the blue and white room. "Do you know, this is the first time I have seen your bedroom, Chérie? I like it; it suits you."

He stripped off his wrinkled jacket and the rest of his clothing followed, until there was an untidy heap on the pale blue carpet. Then he drew her up in front of him and made an erotic ritual of undressing her. The plain, man-tailored shirt and severely cut slacks she had thought appropriate for a farewell scene, he slid sensuously from her body as if they were satin and lace.

When they lay skin to heated skin on the bed, her gaze fastened on the deep violet stains beneath his eyes. She ran her hand over his stubbled cheek and said quietly, "You look so tired, Jean-Claude. If you'd rather not, we don't have to make love."

His laugh was strong and exultant. "You misjudge me, Chérie! Only unconsciousness could keep me from making love to you tonight."

He proceeded to demonstrate. With undisguised urgency, he seared her breasts and belly with his mouth. His hands moved feverishly on her skin, and she caught fire from the heat of his touch. When at last he poised over her, she was trembling for the ultimate intimacy.

He groaned, "Ah, *Dieu!* It seems years instead of weeks since we have been together."

In response, she reached for him, pulling him down onto and into her. His bold thrusts filled all the nooks and crannies in her soul that had emptied during the long weeks of missing him.

At the height of her passion, she ached to tell him

how much she loved him, but deliberately held back for fear he would think she spoke only from the frenzy of the moment. And then Jean-Claude steered her onto the road to ecstasy, leading stride by ecstatic stride to the supreme moment of completion.

Some time later, Sherry lay with her head nestled on his damp chest. "Jean-Claude, there's something I want to tell you."

His eyes were closed; his breathing had already begun to deepen. Idly, he trailed his fingers down her bare arm. "Can it wait until the morning, *ma petite?*" he murmured. "I fear now I really am exhausted."

She burrowed closer against him. "No, I don't think it can wait. But it won't take long. I need to tell you . . ." She paused, then said calmly and deliberately, "I love you, Jean-Claude."

His head snapped up off the pillow. *"Vraiment?* Truly?"

She drew back to look at him and found his eyes eagerly devouring her. "Truly," she told him. "I've loved you for a long time. Almost from the very beginning."

"Ah, Chérie! What a gift you give me!" He gathered her against him and held her close for a long time. Then he began, with subtlety and skill, to arouse her again.

She felt the intoxicating thrust of his erection against her belly and laughingly protested, "I thought you were tired."

His hands molded her breasts, drawing her nipples into tingling loci of desire. "Tired? I am not tired. Whoever told you so was a vicious liar."

"I think . . ." She broke off, gasping as he buried his head between her breasts, his stubbled cheeks erotically abrading her sensitized skin. "I . . . I think it was you, Jean-Claude."

"Never! It could not have been I." His scandalized

exclamation fanned his warm breath over her swelling breasts and she trembled with longing.

"I guess you're right. It wasn't you who mentioned being tired," she said much later, when he had again carried her through the winds of the world and beyond.

He said nothing. His eyes were closed and his chest rose and fell in a steady rhythm. Sherry looked at him with love. "Good night, Jean-Claude," she murmured, and snapped off the light.

She awoke to the tantalizing smell of bacon frying. Jean-Claude looked around the edge of the door and grinned. "Ah, good, you are awake," he said, and promptly disappeared.

He must have brought his suitcase in from his car, for he returned a moment later clean-shaven and wearing faded jeans and a red pullover jersey. He was carrying a breakfast tray. "You have been starving yourself while I have been gone," he said severely. "I must put some flesh back on those lovely bones."

While she ate, he sat companionably on the side of the bed. Afterward, he refused her offer of help cleaning up, but suggested she keep him company in the kitchen.

Clad in her favorite old terry-cloth robe, she perched on a kitchen chair and sipped her second cup of coffee. But as she watched Jean-Claude move about the kitchen, a fraction of her old doubts returned to dim the brightness of the morning.

There were so many things she wanted to know— first among them if this time he planned to stay. Or would there be more plane tickets, more awful surprises, more loneliness and indecision?

Casually—she hoped—she asked, "How was your meeting at JRA, Jean-Claude? Are you doing another movie for them?"

"Yes. A sequel to *Guns and Roses*." He was drying the bowl he had mixed the scrambled eggs in. "But it will not be until next year."

"What will you do in the meantime?" Anxiety spinning through her, she focused on the swirling cream in her coffee.

He waved the dishtowel and said blithely, *"Naturellement,* I will look for something else to score."

"You don't have anything lined up then?"

At the revealing sharpness of her tone, he turned to look at her. "Not for the moment." His smile was slow and lazy. "Why are you so worried, Chérie? Even if it is some time before I work, I will not starve. Besides, I have a Los Angeles agent now. He will be looking for something for me."

"A film here in L.A?" she asked, her voice still edged with anxiety.

"That is my hope."

"But it could be anywhere," she murmured.

He shook his head. "My intent is to make my career here in Los Angeles. Only if I do not succeed will I consider other offers." He stole another look at her and said gently, "Besides, I have just returned, Chérie. It is much too soon to worry about when—or if—I may have to go away again."

It might be too soon, but she couldn't help worrying. What if it turned out that his career forever took him here and there, as lightly as a leaf blown by autumn breezes? How could she bear his absences?

She managed to say, not meaning a word of it, "I suppose you're right. It is too soon to worry."

As March trotted by, Sherry hoped each day to hear Jean-Claude had been engaged for a film in Los Angeles.

His lack of concern frustrated her, but on the whole she managed to keep her anxiety submerged, a task made easier by the sheer joy of being with him.

He didn't officially move into her apartment. But after a week when he spent every night in her bed, it seemed silly for him to continue paying for a hotel room and she said so.

"Purely for economic reasons?" he teased.

"What else?" she responded with a grin.

Daily life became very pleasant. Their lovemaking continued to be fulfilling, with no decline in the intensity of their need for each other. And an extra little fillip of satisfaction was given her by the pleasure she found in her songwriting. Living with Jean-Claude seemed to have unleashed her creativity, and before long she had three new songs to send off to Henri Bonchamps.

Jean-Claude went to meetings with his agent and composed chamber music—just to keep his hand in, he said. He also exercised his culinary skills.

One night, when they had finished another gourmet feast, she ran her finger around the constricting waistband of her once-comfortable jeans and complained, "You have to stop cooking like this every night. I'll turn into Porky Pig."

They were standing at the sink, he washing while she dried. He put down his sponge and cupped a damp hand around her bottom. "This does not feel like Porky Pig to me, but delightfully round and womanly."

"I'm serious," she said reprovingly. "Before long, I won't fit into any of my clothes."

"So much the better," he said with a lecherous waggle of his brows. "Without clothes, you could not go off to work every day. You would have to stay at home ... naked."

"You're still not taking me seriously," she grumbled.

He put the last of the dishes on a rack and dried his hands. "Very well, I will take you seriously if you will do the same for me."

She blinked, surprised. "About what, Jean-Claude?"

"About spending a little less time working." Seeing her frown, he said quickly, "Not that I mean for you to stay at home all day, clothed or unclothed, pleasant though that would be. It is just that now—while I am free—I would enjoy it if we could spend more time together."

She stiffened and was surprised to hear herself say snappishly, "One of us has to work, Jean-Claude."

Recoiling, he stared down at her. "What is this, Chérie? It sounds as if you are angry at me."

She bit her lip. "I didn't mean to say that; it just slipped out."

He came to her and slid his fingers along her cheek and through her hair. "It slipped out because it is something you feel. But you do not understand, Chérie. My lack of work is not yet anything to worry about. I will not starve."

She ignored the soothing motions of his hands. "No, *you* don't understand, Jean-Claude. It's not the financial part of it I'm worrying about. It's just that..."

"Just what, Chérie?" he prompted.

She hesitated, then blurted, "If you don't get a film here soon, you'll have to go away again, won't you?"

His voice was very deep and soft. "Perhaps. But this is a problem to be dealt with when—and if—it happens. Don't worry, Chérie. It will be all right."

She wanted to believe him, and tried so hard that it was only much later she realized they had left the question of her working hours both undiscussed and unresolved.

Oddly enough, the next faint cloud drifted onto her

horizon because of a party Jean-Claude mentioned one morning as he dressed.

"What kind of party?" she asked.

"The head of JRA is throwing it to celebrate the first episode of *Guns and Roses*. For business reasons, I should attend." He picked up his brush and smoothed down the springy waves of his hair. "However, it might even be fun."

"I'd love to go. Give me the date and I'll check with Maggie."

He said nothing, but his mouth took on a revealing twist.

Sherry frowned. "You don't think I should have to check with Maggie, do you?"

"No, I do not. I like Maggie, do not misunderstand me, but I still believe you let her take advantage of you. She has frequently taken time off during the last few weeks; you have told me so yourself."

It was true Maggie had gotten into the habit of taking short vacations, leaving Sherry to mind the store. "I did spend that weekend in Santa Barbara with you, Jean-Claude," she pointed out.

He snorted. "That was nearly two months ago. Surely you are entitled to more time off than that. Why not just tell her you will be unable to work that night?"

"That's not how we operate," she protested. "Maggie and I don't tell each other. We ask."

"You ask. She tells," Jean-Claude insisted. But he came and put his arms around her. "Let's not fight about anything so trivial, Chérie."

In due course, Sherry checked the date of the party with Maggie and was assured her partner was free and could cover any work that came up.

During the next week, Sherry saw less of Jean-Claude

than she liked, although the reason for his absences pleased and relieved her—he was involved in discussions about a new film. But after several dinners and late-night meetings, he came home disappointed and annoyed because the film had gone to an older, better-known composer. Though she told him not to worry, the shadow of his leaving seemed to have moved a little closer.

But when the day of the party arrived, Sherry was resolved not to let anything spoil their fun. She was looking forward to an evening out in Jean-Claude's company, and was secretly dying to get a look at the legendary world of Hollywood high-life.

That morning, she reached the KopyKats office to find Maggie on the phone. "Uh-huh, sure," her partner was saying. "Someone'll be here at five."

"What was that about?" Sherry asked curiously.

Maggie swiveled around in her chair. "Fred Wertz wants us to copy the music for a record date at Sequin tomorrow. The score won't be ready until late this afternoon, so it'll go into night hours." She reached for the phone. "I'll call a couple of assistants, but I'm afraid you'll have to handle this one on your own, partner."

Sherry was too stunned to do anything but stammer, "Wh-what?"

"Yep. Jake's parents are driving in for the weekend. He wants me to meet them." Maggie gave a big grin. "You probably aren't going to believe this, but I think it just might be the lead-in to proposal time."

"But I told you last week—Jean-Claude's taking me to a party tonight."

"Gee, is that tonight?" A wheedling tone crept into Maggie's voice. "Maybe the job'll get done early and you'll still be able to go to the party."

It was in Sherry's mind to grin and bear it, to say,

"Okay, Maggie, it's all right," as she had done so many times before. But Jean-Claude's words came back to her. He was right. She *had* let Maggie take advantage of her.

Something fundamental had changed, she realized. The weeks of being loved by Jean-Claude had made her feel different about herself, entitled to stand up for what she wanted. She looked her partner squarely in the eye. "No, Maggie, I'm afraid that's not how it's going to work this time."

Late that afternoon, Sherry danced into the apartment on buoyant feet to find Jean-Claude sitting on the couch, hidden behind an open newspaper.

"Hello, hello!" she cried.

He lowered the newspaper and smiled. "You're very cheerful today, Chérie."

"Oh, I am. Listen Jean-Claude, I have two things to tell you. Both of them pretty wonderful."

He put the paper on the coffee table and gave her his full attention.

"The first thing is that I had a fight with Maggie today." She paused, still surprised at how easily her partner had given in. "Not a fight, actually. Anyway, I stuck up for myself and it's okay. We're still friends."

He leaped from the couch and hurried toward her. "Good girl! I am proud of you."

Stretching out his arms, he reached to pull her into his embrace, but she slipped away from him. "Wait until you hear the second thing I have to tell you." She waved a slip of paper at him. "See this? It came in the office mail today. It's a check for my songs. I'm a paid song-writer, Jean-Claude!"

"How wonderful! I am overjoyed, *ma petite*." He came toward her, and this time she let him catch her.

Hugging her around the waist, he swung her so her feet flew off the floor and her pleated skirt swirled around her thighs.

When he set her down, she slid her hands up his chest and linked them behind his neck. "Um, Jean-Claude, what time do we have to leave for the party?"

"Not until eight. We have hours yet." His eyes met hers and that was all it took.

Sherry was in the perfect party mood when a uniformed maid admitted them to the Tudor-style mansion in Beverly Hills. Set behind a spacious lawn, the house was the kind of place she had ogled in passing but had never expected to visit.

Beside her, Jean-Claude was handsome in a black tuxedo. A long time in front of the mirror had convinced Sherry she was a fit companion to his elegance. In a little boutique, she had found—amazingly, at a price only a little more than she could afford—a miracle of a dress. Floor length in a delicious lavender, it had a mere slip of a bodice and a slinky skirt, both of them half-concealed by a floaty matching drape. With her hair French-braided, a few tendrils left to cling around her cheeks, it didn't take Jean-Claude to tell her that tonight she was beautiful.

Tell her, he had, however. In the bedroom. In the living room. On the way to the car. And frequently during the drive to Beverly Hills.

And if her lips were slightly swollen and her eyes had the faintly drugged look of a lady who had recently made love, surely no one would be crass enough to comment.

She spent an enjoyable half hour sipping champagne and trying not to gawk too obviously at the many celebrities present. There were beautiful blond starlets, and older, prosperous-looking women wearing what Sherry supposed were Puccis and Guccis and Halstons, though which went on what parts of their anatomies she never had been able to keep straight.

Among the men, Sherry recognized several handsome faces, though none so handsome as Jean-Claude. She was amused to see two not particularly handsome visages belonging to Tweedledum and Tweedledee, as alike as two peas in a pod, despite the fact that one wore a blue tuxedo and the other was more conventionally garbed in black.

Returning from a conversation, Jean-Claude slipped his arm around her waist. "Are you enjoying the party, Chérie?"

"I'm having a wonderful time," she enthused.

He mimed alarm with a horrified lift of his brows. *Mon Dieu!* Does this mean you are developing a taste for the decadent Hollywood lifestyle?"

She pretended to have to consider, then relented. "No, I don't think so. There's an old saying that sums up how I feel, Jean-Claude. It's a nice place to visit, but I wouldn't want to live here."

Letting his breath out with a whoosh, he pretended to wipe perspiration from his brow.

She made her second glass of champagne last until it was time for *Guns and Roses* to air. Jean-Claude slipped his arm through hers as they joined the crowd filing into a room with rows of folding chairs facing a giant TV screen. With a twinkle, he said, "Have you noticed who is not here tonight?"

She smiled. "As far as I can tell, everyone is here— at least enough people to populate a medium-sized suburb. How can I possibly tell who's missing?"

"Think about it, Chérie."

She wrinkled her nose at him. "Is this a game? Okay, I'll play. Let's see. Your old friend Minnie Mouse doesn't seem to be present."

"Very true, Chérie, but that is not who I had in mind."

"The President isn't..." She broke off with sudden comprehension. "Andrew Watson isn't here, is he? What does it mean, Jean-Claude?"

Jean-Claude gave her a delighted conspiratorial look. "What it means, Chérie, is that there is justice in this world. M'sieu Watson's services are no longer required by JRA Films."

They slipped into a pair of seats and Sherry asked, "How did it happen?"

He shrugged. "I am not sure. All I know is that Lumley and Robinson were responsible."

"Who?"

"The two men who were at the recording studio the day of the party."

The lights lowered and a picture formed on the giant TV screen in front of them. "Oh, you mean Tweedledum and Tweedledee," she whispered.

Jean-Claude looked startled. "Who?"

She smiled and patted his knee. "Never mind."

When the first episode of *Guns and Roses* ended, she heard echoes of her own sentiments in the enthusiastic comments of others. "Sure to be up for an Emmy in the miniseries category," someone said.

They were directed to the dining room, where a lavish buffet table had been set up. After they had moved forward a few paces in the line, Jean-Claude was drawn into conversation with the man behind them. At Sherry's elbow, an attractive middle-aged brunette murmured, "What a crowd! I hate these bashes, don't you?"

Sherry considered dissembling, then admitted, "Actually, I'm having a wonderful time, but then it's the first party like this I've ever been to."

The woman smiled. "Your honesty is most refreshing, my dear. What is it that you do?"

"I'm a copy—" She stopped mid-word and proudly corrected herself. "I'm a songwriter." She saw Jean-Claude's head turn at that and a brief smile cross his face.

"Really?" The brunette looked interested. "Would I have heard any of your songs?"

"I doubt it," Sherry admitted. "They're selling a little, but only in Europe."

Soon Jean-Claude joined the conversation, and a few minutes later, the woman drifted away. He looked down at Sherry and said approvingly, "I was pleased to hear you introduce yourself as a songwriter, Chérie."

"I felt like a fraud as soon as I said it," she confessed. "There's only been one check, after all, and it wasn't exactly enormous."

"Perhaps not, but the checks will grow larger in time." He paused, then said slowly, "Have you realized that sooner or later, you will have a decision to make?"

She frowned. "What do you mean, Jean-Claude?"

"You will have to decide between being a copyist and a songwriter, Chérie."

Her frown deepened. It had never crossed her mind that a choice was involved. KopyKats would continue to pay the bills, while songwriting would add a spice of creative satisfaction to her life. But Jean-Claude sounded as if he expected her eventually to give up her business.

Her frown developed a twist of annoyance. She might have known he would expect her to slide into something just as insecure as his own career.

He noticed her expression and said, "You don't have

to decide now, Chérie. Perhaps it is too soon to even mention it."

She opened her mouth to say it certainly was, when a maid in a black and white uniform appeared at her side. "There's a telephone call for you, Miss Seaton."

"For me?"

"Yes, ma'am. You can take it in the study, if you like."

It had to be Maggie, Sherry thought as she followed the maid. No one else knew where she was. But after the talk they'd had, Maggie wouldn't have dreamed of calling for anything less than a conflagration in the KopyKats office.

Alarm uncoiling in her, she pressed the lighted button on the phone and picked it up. "This is Sherry Seaton."

Across the wires came Maggie's voice. "You know, I'd forgotten how much he looks like Cary Grant."

Sherry glared through the phone at her partner. "You didn't call me here to talk about Cary Grant!"

"No. I called about your father."

"What about him?"

"He's here, at the office," Maggie said. "He drove up about three minutes ago."

Chapter 11

"I'M SORRY WE had to leave early," Sherry said.

Jean-Claude steered the car up one of the winding canyon roads that cut through the Santa Monica mountains. "No matter. I had already seen the people I needed to see."

She slanted him a curious glance. "I hadn't realized you were there to see anyone in particular."

"A few producers and others in the industry. It is always wise to let it be known one is available for work."

She tried to keep her tone light. "Do you think anything will come of it?"

He slowed the car to ease around a particularly vicious curve. "Perhaps, perhaps not. It is impossible to know."

Even though she dreaded the answer, she had to ask the question that had hovered around the edges of her thoughts for weeks. "Jean-Claude, what happens if you don't get a film here in L.A.?"

"Sooner or later, I will have to work. Even if I could afford not to, one has to keep active or one's career begins to die." He threw her a quick glance from the corners of his eyes. "Are you sure you wish to discuss this now, Chérie?"

"I'm sure. Go on, tell me more."

He let out a sigh. "Very well. If nothing comes up for me in Los Angeles, I will have to accept one of the offers from France."

She pressed her head against the seatback and stared straight ahead at nothing. "I didn't know you'd had offers from France."

"Oh, yes, there have been several. But I have refused them."

"But you can't keep refusing them," she said slowly.

"Not indefinitely, no."

They had reached the peak of the mountain. Spread out below was a glittering carpet of lights, miles and miles of suburban streets with broader, brighter swaths where major arteries cut through the San Fernando Valley.

Jean-Claude slowed the car and reached over to squeeze her hand. "Don't worry, Chérie. As yet, it has not come to that."

For once, his touch brought her no comfort. Deep within, she had cherished the hope—irrational though she knew it was—that he would assure her he would never leave her again.

As the car curved down the winding road, she fell into a brooding silence. She had to face it. Unless good fortune intervened, Jean-Claude would go away again.

The KopyKats office was blazing with lights. With Jean-Claude on her heels, Sherry pushed open the back door and was unsurprised to find a poker game in progress, with half a dozen men grouped around one end of the long work table.

Maggie stood nearby, biting her lip. When she saw Sherry, she hurried over. "I tried to tell them they couldn't play poker here, but..." She shook her head. "I don't know quite what happened. Your father talked me into it, I guess."

Sherry's grin was wry. "I can imagine. It's okay, though. I'm sure the police wouldn't consider us worth a raid."

At that moment, one of the poker players—indeed bearing a faint resemblance to Cary Grant—looked up from a pile of greenbacks and coins in front of him. "Well, there's my little girl!"

He pushed back his chair, strode over to Sherry, and enfolded her in a bone-crushing hug. Holding her at arm's length, he beamed. "I wouldn't have thought it was possible, but I do believe you've gotten even prettier since the last time I saw you."

A smile tugged at Sherry's lips, and she felt the sting of sentimental tears hazing her vision. "Oh, Daddy, it's really good to see you."

Flying Bill had aged little since his last visit. His face was tanned a healthy bronze, and his body was lean and trim-looking in a well-cut navy-blue blazer. Still focusing on Sherry, he exclaimed, "I can hardly wait to hear all about you, sweetheart, how you've been, what you've been up to..." He seemed for the first time to notice Jean-Claude. "Sorry I interrupted your evening out," he said apologetically. "How about introducing me to your friend?"

Sherry made introductions, and the two men shook hands. After a moment, Flying Bill said to Jean-Claude, "I don't suppose you happen to know anything about poker, do you, son?"

Into Jean-Claude's eyes came the most alarming twinkle. "I think I can claim some small acquaintance with the game."

"How about you, sweetheart?" Flying Bill draped his arm around Sherry's shoulder. "Do you still remember anything your old man taught you about five-card draw?"

"I remember a little," she admitted. "But I think I'd rather not play tonight."

Flying Bill looked only mildly disappointed. "All the better, baby. You can be my good-luck charm." He gave a broad wink. "Looks to me as if I'm going to need one. Jean-Claude looks to me like a pretty lucky fellow."

Jean-Claude's eyes met Flying Bill's, as if the two men had already reached some kind of understanding. "Oh, I am. Very lucky, I assure you, sir."

Maggie said her good-byes and room was made at the table for Sherry and Jean-Claude. When Flying Bill won a big hand, he turned to Sherry with a grin. "I knew you'd be lucky for me, sweetheart. You always have been, you know."

Sherry nodded. She remembered sitting beside her father when she was a child, never bored even when the game went on for hours, endlessly thrilled just because he was there.

But he had always gone away again, she reminded herself, just as he was bound to go away this time. The wistfulness of the thought startled her a little, since she had supposed she had long ago come to terms with Flying Bill's shortcomings.

Her gaze drifted to meet Jean-Claude's and she forced a smile, but he seemed to see through it and asked quietly, "Are you all right, Chérie? Is something wrong?"

Deliberately, she broadened her smile. "Nothing's wrong. I'm fine, Jean-Claude."

The game broke up an hour later, and the other men

departed. "You're a pretty good poker player," Flying Bill announced to Jean-Claude with satisfaction.

Jean-Claude glanced down at the pile of cash on the table in front of him. "My luck held tonight, as I had hoped."

"I'll say it did!" Flying Bill gathered up his winnings, then looked up at Sherry. "Well, baby, it's getting late. I guess it's about time to hit the hay."

Sherry frowned, then smoothed the frown away to say lightly, "Just where were you planning to do your hay-hitting, Dad?"

Flying Bill's face fell. "Why, honey, I don't want to impose, but Maggie said she's not living with you anymore, and if you've got a spare room..."

From behind Flying Bill, Jean-Claude pointed at himself, then jerked his thumb over his shoulder, pantomiming his willingness to disappear.

Sherry shook her head. Even to save her father's feelings, she wouldn't degenerate into hypocrisy. "You're welcome to stay, Dad," she said, "if you're sure you don't mind sharing the apartment with Jean-Claude and me."

A look of dismay crossed Flying Bill's face, but he was quick to recover. "I'd be intruding. Sorry, baby. I shouldn't have asked."

Jean-Claude looked from father to daughter and interjected, "Of course you must stay at the apartment, if that is what both you and Sherry wish."

What Sherry wished, she thought as Jean-Claude drove toward the apartment with Flying Bill's rattletrap Ford following along behind, was what she'd always wished— for her father to be just a little more like other people's fathers.

As if he had read her mind, Jean-Claude said, "You

have never mentioned your father's profession, Chérie. He has something to do with aircraft?"

"Aircraft?" Sherry snorted. "Whatever gave you that idea? Oh! His nickname, I suppose."

"Yes, of course."

She couldn't help laughing. "He's called Flying Bill because he's a high flyer." When Jean-Claude still looked baffled, she explained, "A high flyer is a gambler who takes a lot of chances . . . and sometimes even wins. It's sort of a compliment . . . I think."

"Yes, I understand. Your father gambles. But you still have not told me his profession."

She said gently, "Gambling *is* his profession, Jean-Claude."

It was a few days later when she discovered she had another wish concerning Flying Bill. This time it was that he and Jean-Claude hadn't hit it off quite so chummily. Although she and her father spent some pleasant hours together, catching up on each other's lives, it was with Jean-Claude that he seemed to have a special rapport.

Watching the two men with their heads together, she thought she detected a resemblance between them. It stemmed from nothing so overt as the arrangement of their features or the architecture of their bones, but came from beneath the skin. A matter of attitudes and assumptions shared by both . . . but oh, so different from her own.

One morning at breakfast Flying Bill said, "I was just thinking, honey. Remember how I used to take you to the races when you were a kid?"

She smiled. "Yes, I remember." Those days with her father, watching the beautiful animals fly around the track, were filed among her happiest memories.

"Well, the ponies are running today at Santa Anita. Want to go?"

Sherry swallowed her last bite of crisp blueberry waffle. "Thanks, but I can't, Dad. I have to work."

Flying Bill cast a conspiratorial glance at Jean-Claude. "Sherry always did have her nose to the grindstone more than was good for her. How about you, son? Want to take a flyer on the nags?"

Sherry glanced at Jean-Claude, certain he would refuse, and was surprised to hear him exclaim, "An excellent idea! I have not been to the races since last summer at Deauville."

Her mouth opened, then closed again. Narrowing her eyes, she said, "I didn't know you were a race fan."

"I am not a fan, or only an occasional one. But it is a lovely spring day, Chérie. A perfect day to be out in the open air with the beautiful Thoroughbreds flying down the track. Are you certain you will not change your mind and join us?"

She bit her lip, then blurted, "No, I can't go. And I'm not sure you should, either."

Jean-Claude's eyebrows rose. "Why should I not go, Chérie?"

"I thought you were supposed to see your agent today," she said flatly, and realized her face had formed a thin-lipped mask of disapproval.

Flying Bill shook his head. "Uh-oh! When she does that, she looks just like my sister Martha. Don't let her get in the habit, son, or she'll make your life miserable."

Sherry winced at the thought that she could resemble the stern aunt who had raised her, but found it impossible to soften the muscles around her mouth and eyes.

Jean-Claude winked at Flying Bill. "If you will leave us alone for a few minutes, my friend, I will try to talk her out of her fit of pique."

"Okay. I'll be in my room when you're ready to go."

Their overt collusion was too much for her temper. She threw down her napkin. "Honestly! The pair of you are impossible!" Seizing her plate, she stood and flounced to the sink as her father left the room.

Quick as a flash, Jean-Claude was on his feet. Moving up behind her, he curved his hands gently around her shoulders. "Chérie, Chérie," he murmured in her ear. "Do not be angry. It truly is a lovely day for the races. And besides, if my agent had anything to report, he would have called me."

He pressed a kiss to the base of her throat, and despite her anger, a shiver of delight traveled down her spine. "Jean-Claude, aren't you the slightest bit worried about getting another film?" she asked.

"A little, perhaps. I had hoped for something before now." His warm breath tickled her ear, adding to the sensations whispering through her. "But the next film will come when it will come. And in the meantime, it's a beautiful day for the races."

"I don't see how you can be so calm about it." He was just like her father, she thought with a renewed spurt of anger. Never thinking beyond the moment. Never seeing what his blithe, uncaring attitude did to the people who loved him.

With gentle insistence, he turned her to face him. "Chérie, you must not worry so. Worrying does no good. And besides, as long as we love each other, there is nothing to worry about."

He moved his hands over her ribcage, pulling her

closer. The heat of his body caressed her skin, and the brush of his muscled thighs did all kinds of delightful things to her innards.

He said in a soft, husky voice, "You do love me, don't you, Chérie?"

"I suppose," she grumbled.

He ran his hands down her back and over her bottom. "You will have to do better than that, Chérie."

She was beginning to have trouble breathing. In a husky voice, she admitted, "Of course I love you."

He pulled her forward, pressing her lower body into the cradle of his hips, his hands kneading deep into her buttocks. "That is much better, Chérie. I love you, too. Very much."

With a little sigh, she gave in, raising her face for his kiss. The first intimate plunge of his tongue was enough to ignite her. Hungrily returning his kisses, she rubbed her body provocatively against him.

He shifted his hands so they covered her breasts. The expression in his eyes made her pulse race. "I have just had a brilliant idea, Chérie. I will tell your father I cannot go to the races, after all. We will spend the day at home . . . alone."

For one insane moment, she was tempted, then caught herself. Stiffening, she said coldly, "You may not have anything better to do, but I have to go to work."

He dropped his hands from her body and stepped back, angry sparks glinting in his eyes. "You question how I spend my time? Has it occurred to you that I might also question your use of yours?"

"How could you?" she demanded defensively.

He put his hands on his hips and glared at her. "Very easily. Have I not told you that I want—and need—to spend more time with you than your work allows?"

He had mentioned it before, she remembered, but she had put it out of her mind. She would have enjoyed spending more time with him, too, but work was a fact of life, not something to be tampered with on a whim.

Jean-Claude rolled on inexorably, "And if that is not a consideration, then think of the fact that your work also occupies much of the time you might be using to write songs."

She turned her head away, refusing to look at him. "Writing songs is only a hobby."

"It *was* a hobby, perhaps, but you are a professional now, Chérie."

"One check doesn't make it a career," she protested.

"Perhaps not now, but soon, if you dedicate yourself, if you are willing to spend the time it requires to develop your talent."

She faced him with accusation in her face and voice. "Just what are you suggesting, Jean-Claude?"

"I am suggesting that is is time for you to consider ridding yourself of KopyKats."

She had known that was coming ever since the night of the party. But the idea was absurd. It made no sense at all. Jean-Claude knew he might soon have to go away again. Did he expect her to cast herself adrift from the one stable element in her life?

The gulf in their understanding of each other yawned so wide that she had no idea how to talk to him across it. In the end, she simply shook her head.

At that moment, Flying Bill stuck his head in the kitchen door. "Haven't you got her gentled down yet, son?"

Jean-Claude gave her a long look. "Will you at least think about it, Chérie?"

Again, she shook her head.

His eyes held hers. For a moment, she thought he was going to say something else, but he merely shrugged and turned to Flying Bill. "Let us go, my friend."

After the two men left the apartment, Sherry hurried off to work. But throughout the day, she was preoccupied, thinking about Jean-Claude. Bit by bit, her old fears revived. Her sad conclusion was that she had been living in a dream world all these weeks.

Not only did the specter of his leaving grow more fully fleshed each day, but his suggesting she give up KopyKats was a symptom—though not the only one—of the differences heaped up like an unbreachable wall between them.

Something had to happen.

It seemed almost predestined when, the next morning, Flying Bill announced he was leaving. Looking up from his ham and eggs, he said casually, "Your hospitality's been terrific, sweetheart, but I thought I'd take off this morning and head for Vegas."

Sherry put down her coffee cup, startled to discover tears stinging her eyelids. She blinked hard to clear her vision and said, "Do you really have to go so soon, Dad? You've only been here a few days."

"Still, I have to go, sweet potato," he said, seemingly oblivious to her pain. "I've been in your way long enough."

Though Jean-Claude joined in Sherry's attempts to convince him, Flying Bill remained adamant. At the door of the apartment, he caught Sherry in a last embrace. Gruffly, as if embarrassed, he said, "I'm so glad we had this little visit." He cleared his throat and looked out over the top of her head. "I know I never was much of a father to you, sweetheart. I always meant to do better, but somehow I never managed it. Anyway, it means a lot to

me to see you settled down with a nice young fellow like
Jean-Claude."

Settled, Sherry echoed ironically after she kissed her
father good-bye. How could the word apply, when she
felt, deep inside, as if everything was rolling downhill
toward inevitable disaster?

The crash came, as she had known it eventually must,
that very night. Jean-Claude fixed a luscious dinner, but
neither the meal nor his efforts at conversation did much
to lighten her depression.

In the living room, he drew her down beside him on
the couch, then was silent for so long that her nerves
began prickling with apprehension. Finally, he said,
"Chérie, I have vowed not to make the same mistake I
made with you before."

Dismay uncoiled in her. "I don't understand what you
mean, Jean-Claude," she said, though she was very much
afraid she did.

He took her hand and pressed it against his cheek. "I
have vowed never again to withhold information from
you, not even for a day. I saw my agent this morning.
There is the possibility of a film in New York." He
paused, then corrected himself. "No, it is more than a
possibility. It is, I am told, a near certainty."

That he might go to New York had never occurred to
her. She had thought of France if—no, when—he had
to go. But of course, films were made in New York as
well as in Los Angeles. With a trace of hysteria, she
thought, *There's no end to the places he can go . . . leaving me alone.*

She dropped her gaze to the pleated scarlet caftan she
had slipped into when she got home from work. "How
long will you be gone?'

"Most likely only a few days this time. But once I

start the film, I will be away for several weeks."

Sherry felt an empty place gape inside her. Weeks could turn to months, as she knew all too well.

He slid his hand under her hair to warm the side of her neck. "Do not look so sad, Chérie."

She swallowed and said glumly, "I can't seem to help it."

Searching her face, he said slowly, "There is a solution, you know."

She gave a quick, blind shake of her head. "I can't think of any."

"Look at me, Chérie."

Reluctantly, she did as he asked. His eyes locked with hers and he said with rising urgency, "Come to New York with me. If not this first time, at least when I go to score the film."

"You know I can't do that."

"Explain to me why you cannot," he persisted.

She spoke with the strained patience one uses with a child who is being deliberately obtuse. "You know why. Because I have to work."

"You do not *have* to do anything," he said brusquely. "We have spoken before about the need for you to one day divest yourself of KopyKats. This merely advances that time."

She set her jaw and said through gritted teeth, "You're talking nonsense, Jean-Claude. What makes you think I'd ever agree to sell KopyKats? It's my business. Maggie and I built it up from scratch."

"But it is not a business that satisfies you. You have said enough for me to know that."

"It pays the rent," she said defensively.

"And that is all that matters?"

"Not all. But it certainly is important."

His voice grated alarmingly on her ears. "More important than your songwriting? More important than our being together?"

Anger spurted through her. He was trying to manipulate her into giving up the one firm rock in a world of shifting insecurities.

She had memorized so well the speech she had once planned to deliver, that now the words sprang to her lips with appalling ease. Pulling stiffly away from him, she said. "I'm sorry, Jean-Claude. This just won't work out. There are too many problems between us. You know how I feel about long-distance relationships."

He said roughly, "I've already told you how we may solve that problem, Chérie."

"But don't you see? Your so-called solution just points up all the other problems. We just don't think the same way, Jean-Claude. We're too different in our values and expectations. I've told you that from the beginning."

Deep down, she had cherished a flame of hope that Jean-Claude would counter with an insistence that she was wrong and would go on to produce answers to their problems that she could accept.

But instead of calmly and reasonably demolishing her objections, he surged to his feet, fury roiling in his face. A remote part of her noted that she had never seen him really angry before. The blaze in his eyes was daunting.

He planted his hands on his hips and stormed at her, "Yes, you are right. From the first, you have insisted in every way you could that you and I were not right for each other."

She averted her eyes from the churning emotions in his and insisted, "You know it's true."

"I know nothing of the sort," he countered. In three long strides, he crossed the room where he stared out the window at a black sky, seemingly struggling to master himself. Finally, he said in a quieter voice, "Have you ever heard of a self-fulfilling prophecy, Chérie?"

"Yes, of course. That's where you think something is going to happen and then unconsciously make it turn out the way you expect." She shook her head in disbelief. "You think that's what I'm doing? It's not true. It's just that I've known from the beginning it couldn't work. You must see it, too."

"Do you know what I see?" He whirled from the window, his face a grim mask. "I see that from the first I have battled with you for our love until I am tired of battling." His shoulders slumped, his eyes dulled, and he said with slow deliberation, "In truth, I am exhausted from struggling with you."

She said bitterly, "Then why don't you just give up?"

Anger flared in his eyes, and he stalked across the room to her. Dropping his hands on her shoulders, he gave her a convulsive little shake. "If I thought it would do any good, I would shake you until I had shaken some sense into that pretty, but stubborn head of yours. I would shake you until you admitted that you and I were meant to be together, through this life and beyond." He froze with his hands on her shoulders, then dropped his arms to his sides and stepped back a pace. In a remote, cold voice, he finished, "But it would not help. You would only continue to fight me."

In his eyes, she saw no tenderness but a mixture of other things—disappointment, anger, and bitterness. She flinched from his gaze and said weakly, "Jean-Claude, you don't understand."

"I do understand," he insisted. "I understand that you are a coward. You want a safe, secure life. You want to hang on to a business that stifles you. Further, you want a man who is the same as you. Someone whose life is circumscribed by work and duty. Someone content never to adventure. Someone who comes home at the same time each and every night."

His words struck a chord of memory and she murmured, "An accountant . . . or a dentist."

He rounded on her. "So, you *admit* that is what you want."

She lifted her chin and said with a last spurt of defensiveness, "Yes, that's exactly what I want. And why not? There's nothing wrong with wanting stability."

"No. There is nothing wrong . . ." His laugh was a bitter rasp. ". . . if you are willing to do without joy and to do without love." He stepped back another pace, as if he needed to distance himself from her. In a voice laden with scorn, he flung at her, "Find your little accountant or dentist if that is what you desire. I wish you good luck, for I tell you this, Chérie, I will not fight for you anymore."

Turning on one heel, he walked to the door. There he paused. With one hand on the knob, he said, "I will send someone to pick up my things in the morning." Then, with a quiet finality, he shut the door behind him.

She stared at the space in the air where he had been and tried to feel victorious. No longer would she have to worry about how different they were from each other. No longer would she have to fear the day when he would leave her. At last she had gained what she knew was for the best.

But it was a funny kind of victory. To celebrate, she cried until her throat hurt and her eyes were swollen. She cried until her heart felt dry and shriveled, like something long dead. And who would bring it back to life again, she wondered once her tears were spent, now that Jean-Claude was gone?

Chapter 12

FIRST THING THE next morning, Sherry started trying to pick up the pieces of her life. She faced a difficult moment when her doorbell rang and a young man wearing the cap of a crosstown messenger service said, "I'm supposed to pick up some luggage at this address."

She had already packed Jean-Claude's things, blinking away tears as she folded his jeans and pullovers and tucked his razor into a corner of his suitcase. She handed his luggage over to the messenger with an awful sense of finality—it really was over.

Another bad moment came when Henri Bonchamps telephoned and echoed some of Jean-Claude's words. "I need more of your songs, Mademoiselle Seaton, six or eight at a time, not three. There is beginning to be a demand for your work, and at present I cannot fill it."

She promised to try, but her creativity seemed to have fled with Jean-Claude. Though she spent many hours with her guitar, nothing happened, not even a pathetic heartbreaker of a song to match her emotions.

Bit by bit, she began to sort things out and realized

Jean-Claude was right about some of it. She *had* decided, early on, that their relationship could never work. With some of the things she had thought and said, she *had* been acting out a self-fulfilling prophecy.

Fate hadn't helped, she also concluded. The trick of timing that had ordained Jean-Claude's announcement so close on the heels of her father's departure had made her overreact.

But two problems still seemed insoluble. One was the difficulty of coping with an absentee lover. But even that one might have been solved—though she couldn't see how, exactly—if Jean-Claude hadn't tried to force her to get rid of KopyKats. The day might come when she would be willing, but it had been wrong of him to push her before she was ready.

Half a dozen times during those days, she considered calling his agent, the one person who might be able to tell her where Jean-Claude was, but each time she decided against it. Considering the grim finality with which he had left, she was certain she could do nothing to change his mind. And even if she could have waved a magic wand and taken their relationship back to what it was, nothing fundamental would have been solved.

The hours limped by until, finally, a week and a day had passed without Jean-Claude. On a Saturday afternoon, Sherry sat in her living room, trying to decide what to do. She had given up songwriting for the time being. The apartment was so spick and span she feared wearing the finish off the wooden surfaces. Her hair was squeaky clean and her nails freshly manicured.

She had just decided to take a walk when she heard the tramp of feet in the hall. Many feet.

She sat bolt upright. Burglars? A large troupe of them was just barely imaginable, but at two o'clock in the afternoon?

A muffled voice from outside said, "Now, boss?" and the doorbell rang.

Frowning a little, she went to the door. Leaving the chain on, she peered out through the two-inch opening at a face painted with bold lines of red and white surrounding a bulbous nose. Above the face was a ruffled cap, below it baggy, polka-dotted clothing.

A clown? In her hallway? "Yes?" she inquired.

"Got a message to deliver for Sherry Seaton," the clown said.

It must be one of those funny telegram services. At once, her heart accelerated and a surge of hope threatened her breathing. Could the clown have been sent by Jean-Claude? A tremulous smile curved her lips. It was just the crazy kind of thing he'd do, but . . .

Cautioning herself against hoping for too much, she unhooked the chain, opened the door wide, and gasped. There was not one clown but eight, spread out in a line in the hall.

A chuckle burst out of her, and along with it came the first lightness of spirit she had experienced since Jean-Claude's departure. Eight clowns *had* to be from him. Who else would do something so absurd?

The lead clown said, "You ready, lady?"

"I sure am."

"One and-a two and-a three." In unison—or semi-unison—the members of the bizarre chorus line broke into a clumsy little shuffling dance. Their red grease-painted mouths opened. To the tune "Harvest Moon," they sang:

> *"Sherry, we broke up*
> *And now, I'm feeling sad.*
> *Can't we try again, because*
> *I just keep on thinking of the love that we had."*

There was considerably more in this vein, each line of doggerel worse than the one before. By the end, Sherry was helpless with laughter.

But not too helpless to have noticed one voice—a deep baritone—that sounded familiar. She traced it to its source, the clown on the far right end of the line. He, unlike his fellows, wore a clown mask instead of grease-paint, though his suit was as baggy, his cap as foolish as those of the others.

Her first impulse was to rush out into the hall and throw her arms around him, but caution made her hold back. What good would it do for Jean-Claude to return if there was still no solution to their problems? Besides, she had a perverse urge to see how far he would go.

The clowns came to a rather muddled end of their ditty. Carefully keeping her eyes away from the end clown, she said to their leader, "Is that it? Or do you have any more in your repertoire?"

The clowns groaned. Their leader said with deter-mined cheerfulness, "We rehearsed a couple more, but we were kinda hoping you wouldn't want to hear them." With a glance at the end clown, he asked, "What do you want us to do now, boss?"

With a flourish, the end clown pulled off his cap and slipped his mask up to the top of his head. "Chérie, it is I, Jean-Claude." Despite his foolery, his face was grave.

She made her eyes go round with astonishment. "Why, Jean-Claude! What a surprise seeing you here. Have you taken up a new profession?"

It was the first time she had ever seen him look flustered. Ignoring her question, he said, "Do you not, perhaps, have a response to my message?"

She pretended to consider. "Give me a few days to work out a suitable set of lyrics and I'll get in touch."

The lead clown said, "Well, boss, I guess you'd better do your stuff. This lady's a tough nut to crack."

"Indeed she is," Jean-Claude said wryly. "Why do you think I have gone to such lengths as these?" Deftly, he stripped off his clown costume. Beneath was a gray three-piece suit—ultraconservative—with a gray tie.

Now Sherry's astonishment was genuine. "I've never seen you in a suit before. And a three-piece suit at that! You look just like Tweedledum and Tweedledee." She decided not to point out that the effect was somewhat marred by the clown mask still perched on the top of his head.

"Dieu, I hope not." He came to the center of the line. "The suit is symbolic of the new Jean-Claude." He sank to his knees in front of her. With his hands clasped before his face, he intoned, "Very well, Chérie. I am desperate. Marry me and I promise to be serious at all times. I will think of nothing but duty. I will work twenty-four hours a day."

The lead clown looked uncomfortable. "You don't really mean that, do you, boss?"

"Shh!" Sherry hushed him. "I want to hear this."

Jean-Claude cast the clown a scathing look and proceeded, "I will become a model of all the deadliest virtues. I will consider responsibility at all times. I will come home from work promptly at five every day." He cast her an appealing look. "I am running out of declarations, Chérie. Do you believe me?"

"Not a word," she said blithely. "However, I think

you'd better come in where we can discuss it without your friends."

The lead clown clapped Jean-Claude on the shoulder. "Attaway, boss! Well, we'll be taking off, now. If you ever need our services again, just..."

Jean-Claude silenced him with a glare. The next instant, he was off his knees and inside the apartment with the door shut behind him.

Belatedly, he seemed to become aware of the mask perched on top of his head. He pulled it off and tossed it to the floor. With great determination, he advanced on her, his arms spread wide.

Though tempted to slip into his embrace and simply glory in his return, she got a grip on herself. "Whoa! Not so fast."

His face fell. "But, Chérie..."

She looked at him with love, but forced herself to say slowly, "Why did you come, Jean-Claude?"

His eyes were serious and intent. "Because I love you. Because I cannot bear that we parted in anger. Because I want you beside me every minute of every day for the rest of our lives. Because I am willing to do whatever is necessary to make it right between us." A hopeful smile lightened the gravity of his face. "Will those reasons do for a start, Chérie?"

"I think they'll do quite well." She felt as if she were glowing, lit from inside by an incandescent flame. If he really meant the commitment he had just made, then there simply *had* to be a solution to their problems.

He looked momentarily abashed. "I am sorry for the manner in which we parted. I should not have lost my temper, Chérie."

He reached for her hand and touched it briefly with his fingertips. The air seemed to sizzle with electricity, and she stammered, "Wh-why did you bother with the clowns?"

A faint smile flickered across his face. "Ah, that! The clowns were because, a long time ago, I discovered that humor works with you where seriousness does not."

"So you were preying on my weaknesses!"

He nodded. "I had to find some way of breaking down your defenses." His expression grew earnestly imploring. "Can we talk seriously, Chérie?"

"Of course." She gestured at the couch, thinking how odd it was to be formal with Jean-Claude. And yet, until they had talked, until they had made a serious effort to solve their problems, she could not go into his arms as she longed to do.

He sat beside her on the couch, his shoulders hunched, his hands falling loosely between his knees, and his eyes focused on the russet carpet. After a brief silence, he said, "I must acknowledge that I was wrong to push you to give up KopyKats. Just because I can live with uncertainty does not mean you should have to."

She could see this was difficult for him. In an effort to make it easier, she touched his shoulder and was glad when he snapped his head around, his eyes lighting as they fell on her.

"Yes, you were wrong to push me," she said gently. "But you were right in a way, too. Probably I will have to sell out eventually." She paused and said judiciously, "I'm not ready to do that yet, but I have told Maggie we need to hire someone part-time so I can take time off for songwriting. And . . ."

"And?" he prompted.

"And just to spend time with you, if it works out that way," she finished.

He smiled, then said seriously, "If that is the way you

wish it, Chérie. You have my promise never again to push you toward anything that does not feel right to you."

"That's very fair." She lifted her chin. "Now it's my turn to tell you something." She paused, then hurried out with, "It's taken me all week to figure out you were right about my acting out a self-fulfilling prophecy."

He rested his hand on her shoulder, rubbing gently. "It's all right Chérie. As long as you realize—"

"Wait, there's more. When my father left, I'm afraid I flipped back into childhood for a while. I felt as if you were both abandoning me at once." She drew a deep breath, thinking of the most important lesson she had learned from the past week—that doing without Jean-Claude from time to time was infinitely better than doing without him forever. "If your career takes you away now, I think I can learn to handle it."

"But you will not have to," he interjected. "Not for a while, at least." He captured her hand in his and said eagerly, "The most important thing I have to tell you is this: While in New York, I signed a contract to do three films—but I insisted that the films be done here in L.A."

She gazed at him in disbelief. "Insisted? Wasn't that taking an awful chance?"

He shrugged. "Perhaps, but the chance of losing you was a much more terrible one."

"Oh, Jean-Claude," she breathed, overwhelmed that he would have risked his career for her sake. If that wasn't commitment, she didn't know what the word meant.

He pressed the back of her hand against his cheek and cautioned her, "I can't promise I won't have to be gone some time in the future. But for the next year, at least, I will be here in L.A." A question lit in his eyes and he said slowly, "Unless I could persuade you to take our honeymoon in France?"

Sherry gaped at him. "Honeymoon! But, Jean-Claude, you haven't even proposed."

"But I did!" he insisted with fierce indignation. "Outside in the hall. I was even on my knees in proper fashion."

Had he proposed? Maybe he had at that. So many emotions had swirled through her heart, so many thoughts through her head, it was possible some of his words had slipped past without sinking in. "Drat! I must have missed it."

"In that case, I will have to do it again." He cast her an appealing glance. "Do I have to kneel this time?"

"I don't think that will be necessary. We wouldn't want you to wear holes in the knees of your brand-new suit."

He looked at her. "Chérie, will you—"

"Wait," she interrupted.

"But I was proposing."

"First, Jean-Claude, about all those things you promised out there in the hall. You didn't really mean them, did you?"

"I mean to try." He gave a sheepish grin. "Of course, I am but human, so I cannot promise to succeed."

She exhaled a gusty sigh. "That's a relief. If you really intended to do all that, you might as well not propose."

"No? And why not, pray tell?"

"Because I couldn't possibly marry you." She chose her words carefully. "Why, if you really did all those things you'd be just like any old accountant . . . or a dentist."

The joyous smile on Jean-Claude's face was too much to resist. She swayed toward him and he swept his arms

around her. Before he kissed her, he looked deep into
her eyes and sighed. "Ah, Chérie, I was so afraid . . ."

He let his voice trail away, but she knew what he
meant. "I was, too, Jean-Claude."

His lips met hers in an explosion of passion and promise so overwhelming that a long time later, when she lay
contentedly in his arms, she could not remember how
they had gotten to the bedroom. Magic, she thought.
Jean-Claude's magic.

She let out a little chuckle. "Those clowns! That was
really funny, Jean-Claude."

"I am glad you enjoyed them, Chérie." He paused,
then said, "But here is one thing that is no laughing
matter."

He sounded so serious that she pulled back for a good
look at his face. Seeing a worried frown creasing his
brow, she felt alarmed. What could be wrong now?

"What's the matter?" she demanded.

"It is the question of our wedding. I would like it to
be within the week so we can honeymoon in France
before I start the first film. Do you suppose you can
locate your father in time for him to see us married?"

She smiled, pleased he had thought of including Flying
Bill, and said with assurance, "If I have to, I'll have him
paged in every casino in Las Vegas." She paused, then
added, "The downtown ones, of course. Fortunately, I
won't have to bother with the Strip. He'd never go there."

"Why not?"

Feigning shock at his ignorance, she said, "Because
the odds are much better downtown, of course. Everyone
knows that."

"Hm." He frowned. "What else do you know about
gambling?"

"Well, let's see . . . In a pinch, I can do a pretty good

job of handicapping. Horses, that is. I've never figured out the dog races."

He wrapped his arms around her, hugging her close. *"Mon Dieu!* There are facets of you I never suspected."

She struggled out of his embrace to reach for the phone on the nightstand, but Jean-Claude caught her arm. "What are you doing, Chérie?"

"Why, calling my father, of course. It might take a while to find him."

"Can't it wait for a little?" His voice was plaintive and he ran his hand tantalizingly over her bare hip. "Those facets of you I mentioned? Some of them I would like to discover without delay."

She hesitated with her hand still on the phone, then made up her mind. As she melted into his embrace, she said softly, "Yes, it can wait, Jean-Claude. Everything can wait."

Epilogue

"LISTEN TO THIS, Jean-Claude," Sherry said, and began to read aloud an excerpt from the "Hollywood Gal" column of the *Los Angeles Chronicle*.

"'Seen at the Oscar's: Composer Jean-Claude Delacroix and his lovely wife, Sherry. Jean-Claude narrowly missed out on an Oscar this year, losing to perennial winner John Williams. But rumor has it that Jean-Claude's latest score may give John cause to worry.

"'Songwriter Sherry Delacroix, looking elegant in emerald silk, confided that her songs are doing well in Europe and that she anticipates her first American release sometime next month.'

"I didn't confide any such thing," Sherry said indignantly. "I never even talked to that woman."

Jean-Claude looked up from his section of the newspaper. They were sitting in the sunny breakfast room of their new house. Although they had been married for nearly a year, they had moved only a month before—it had taken time to find a house with studio space for two musicians. "But it's all true, Chérie," he said. "So what difference does it make?"

"None, I suppose." She smiled. "Hollywood Gal said I was elegant. I like that."

"You were, Chérie."

She glanced down at the small bulge in her tummy where their child was growing. "It's a good thing the Oscars happened when they did. I won't be elegant much longer."

Between moving, discovering she was pregnant, and arranging to sell her share of KopyKats to their most trusted assistant, the last months had been hectic. But now she could settle down to songwriting, awaiting the baby's birth . . . and loving Jean-Claude.

He put down his paper and rose from his chair. Standing behind her, he rested his hands on her shoulders, then slid them down over her ripening breasts. "But you are growing more beautiful every day, Chérie."

"Flatterer," she teased; then, suddenly, she frowned. "I just thought of something, Jean-Claude. Here I am, pregnant with your child, and you never did actually propose."

"I did so," he insisted.

"But I didn't hear it."

His hands were still curved lovingly over her breasts. With a heavy sigh, he said resignedly, "Very well, Chérie. I suppose I have no choice but to humor a pregnant woman." There in the kitchen, beside her chair, he sank to his knees and said formally, "Mrs. Delacroix, will you marry me?"

Sherry pretended to examine her nails with great interest. "Hm. Let me think about it."

He rose on one knee and slid his arms around her

waist. His lips nudged the peak of her breast, the nipple already pouting through her T-shirt. "Give me the answer I want, Chérie, or I will stop what I am doing."

A pulse was throbbing low in her body; sweet sensation blossomed from where his mouth warmed her breast. "No, don't stop," she said breathlessly.

He backed off an inch, his lips pressed firmly together, his face implacable.

She wove her fingers through his thick, springy hair and said with a helpless sigh, "All right, I give in. My answer is yes."

SECOND CHANCE AT LOVE

COMING NEXT MONTH

SECOND CHANCE AT LOVE

Be Sure to Read These New Releases!

NO MORE MR. NICE GUY #340 by Jeanne Grant
Thinking his fiancée Carroll finds him tame
and predictable, Alan sweeps her away with dashing
recklessness and exotic romance—to her secret
delight...but ultimate dismay!

A PLACE IN THE SUN #341 by Katherine Granger
Libby Peterson hires casual drifter Rush Mason as
groundskeeper for her Cape Cod inn, not anticipating
the exquisite tension provoked by his unexplained
past...or the undisguised passion in his bold gaze.

A PRINCE AMONG MEN #342 by Sherryl Woods
The joke's on mime Erin Matthews when
the devastating man she's spoofing scoops her into
his arms, dubs her his princess—and gives
her ten days to plan their wedding!

NAUGHTY AND NICE #343 by Jan Mathews
Respectable Cindy Marshall's got scars from
when she stripped for a living, and she doesn't need a
man to mess things up now—especially not cool,
compelling vice squad cop Brad Jordan!

ALL THE RIGHT MOVES #344 by Linda Raye
Coach Ryan McFadden is a *big* man, but
five-feet-eleven referee Lauren Nickels is every inch
his equal—whether they're battling it out on
the basketball court...or volleying sexy innuendos.

BLUE SKIES, GOLDEN DREAMS #345 by Kelly Adams
Joe Dancy appears to be an easygoing farmer
with golden good looks and a string of women after him.
Yet Sara Scott's convinced he's after something:
her money...or her heart?

Order on opposite page

SECOND CHANCE AT LOVE

___ 0-425-08851-0	**MR. OCTOBER #317** Carole Buck	$2.25
___ 0-425-08852-9	**ONE STEP TO PARADISE #318** Jasmine Craig	$2.25
___ 0-425-08853-7	**TEMPTING PATIENCE #319** Christina Dair	$2.25
___ 0-425-08854-5	**ALMOST LIKE BEING IN LOVE #320** Betsy Osborne	$2.25
___ 0-425-08855-3	**ON CLOUD NINE #321** Jean Kent	$2.25
___ 0-425-08908-8	**BELONGING TO TAYLOR #322** Kay Robbins	$2.25
___ 0-425-08909-6	**ANYWHERE AND ALWAYS #323** Lee Williams	$2.25
___ 0-425-08910-X	**FORTUNE'S CHOICE #324** Elissa Curry	$2.25
___ 0-425-08911-8	**LADY ON THE LINE #325** Cait Logan	$2.25
___ 0-425-08948-7	**A KISS AWAY #326** Sherryl Woods	$2.25
___ 0-425-08949-5	**PLAY IT AGAIN, SAM #327** Petra Diamond	$2.25
___ 0-425-08966-5	**SNOWFLAME #328** Christa Merlin	$2.25
___ 0-425-08967-3	**BRINGING UP BABY #329** Diana Morgan	$2.25
___ 0-425-08968-1	**DILLON'S PROMISE #330** Cinda Richards	$2.25
___ 0-425-08969-X	**BE MINE, VALENTINE #331** Hilary Cole	$2.25
___ 0-425-08970-3	**SOUTHERN COMFORT #332** Kit Windham	$2.25
___ 0-425-08971-1	**NO PLACE FOR A LADY #333** Cassie Miles	$2.25
___ 0-425-09117-1	**SWANN'S SONG #334** Carole Buck	$2.25
___ 0-425-09118-X	**STOLEN KISSES #335** Liz Grady	$2.25
___ 0-425-09119-8	**GOLDEN GIRL #336** Jacqueline Topaz	$2.25
___ 0-425-09120-1	**SMILES OF A SUMMER NIGHT #337** Delaney Devers	$2.25
___ 0-425-09121-X	**DESTINY'S DARLING #338** Adrienne Edwards	$2.25
___ 0-425-09122-8	**WILD AND WONDERFUL #339** Lee Williams	$2.25
___ 0-425-09157-0	**NO MORE MR. NICE GUY #340** Jeanne Grant	$2.25
___ 0-425-09158-9	**A PLACE IN THE SUN #341** Katherine Granger	$2.25
___ 0-425-09159-7	**A PRINCE AMONG MEN #342** Sherryl Woods	$2.25
___ 0-425-09160-0	**NAUGHTY AND NICE #343** Jan Mathews	$2.25
___ 0-425-09161-9	**ALL THE RIGHT MOVES #344** Linda Raye	$2.25
___ 0-425-09162-7	**BLUE SKIES, GOLDEN DREAMS #345** Kelly Adams	$2.25
___ 0-425-09284-4	**TANGLING WITH WEBB #346** Laine Allen	$2.25
___ 0-425-09285-2	**FRENCHMAN'S KISS #347** Kerry Price	$2.25
___ 0-425-09286-0	**KID AT HEART #348** Aimée Duvall	$2.25
___ 0-425-09287-9	**MY WILD IRISH ROGUE #349** Helen Carter	$2.25
___ 0-425-09288-7	**HAPPILY EVER AFTER #350** Carole Buck	$2.25
___ 0-425-09289-5	**TENDER TREASON #351** Karen Keast	$2.25